A Dragon Used to Live Here

A Dragon Used to Live Here

Annette LeBlanc Cate

CANDLEWICK PRESS

Copyright © 2022 by Annette LeBlanc Cate

First edition 2022

Library of Congress Catalog Card Number 2021946745
ISBN 978-1-5362-0451-3

22 23 24 25 26 27 LBM 10 9 8 7 6 5 4 3 2 1

Printed in Melrose Park, IL, USA

This book was typeset in Archetype.
The illustrations were done in ink.

Candlewick Press
99 Dover Street
Somerville, Massachusetts 02144

www.candlewick.com

A JUNIOR LIBRARY GUILD SELECTION

for Cathy

Chapter One

I don't know, Thomas," said Emily, squinting into the bright morning sun. "Something here doesn't look quite right."

"It's *fine*, Emily," her brother said. He selected an arrow from his quiver and fit it to his bowstring.

"I just don't know," she said again. "It feels like maybe the angle is wrong."

With two fingers, Thomas pulled the string back slowly and held it by his ear, as he had been taught. "It looks exactly like it always does. We set up just like the archery master always docs: exactly seventy-five paces from the target, which I'm about to hit, just like usual." He closed one eye, aiming carefully.

"Still looks funny to me," said Emily. Then her face brightened. "Hey, I know what's wrong! It's usually seventy-five of *his* paces! He's way taller than us! We're too close!"

She was right, but it was too late. They both watched the arrow sail cleanly over the straw target, missing it by a good three feet at least, and land somewhere in the mess of tangled bushes at the base of the stone tower that stood across the courtyard.

"Oops," said Thomas.

Emily sighed loudly. "I *told* you we shouldn't have started without the archery master! And now we've lost one of the good arrows. You really shouldn't have started with one of the good ones, Thomas."

"It's not lost! It's just over there in those bushes." Thomas turned and stomped through the long grass toward the tower, with Emily following.

"I'm sure it's here somewhere," he muttered as he pushed aside some of the branches. "Oh, great, they're prickly!"

Emily peered underneath. "I don't see it anywhere."

"It was an extremely long shot. It must have gone in deep." Thomas pushed through the bushes a little farther. "Hey, did you know there was a window here? There must be a basement room in the tower."

Emily, still looking for the arrow, did not answer.

"Most likely my arrow went right through the window," Thomas continued. "I didn't hear any screaming, though, so I probably didn't kill anyone . . ."

"They wouldn't be screaming if they were *dead*," Emily pointed out.

"I suppose," said Thomas. "There's a curtain in the window, so I can't see anything. But it *was* a powerful arrow."

"It really wasn't," said Emily. She looked around at the wall surrounding the empty courtyard. "There isn't anyone out here anyway, right? I mean, aren't the towers just for the guards? Who would be in the basement?"

"I have no idea," said Thomas. The children seldom visited the outer wall of the castle. Like most everyone else, they lived in the keep, which was the fortress situated safely inside the inner wall, where most of the castle's day-to-day business took place. The grassy courtyard between the inner and outer walls was mostly reserved for archery, horseback riding, falconry, and other activities their mother considered dangerous.

"Helloooooooo!" Emily called through the window.

All remained quiet.

"I'm going to crawl through," said Thomas.

"A well-brought-up young lady always tries the door before the window," Emily said primly.

"I'm not a well-brought-up young lady," said Thomas.

"Okay, think of the prickles, then," said Emily.

"You're right," Thomas agreed. "Let's try the door. Funny we've never noticed it all these years!"

The door was on the other side of the tower, down a few stone steps, and almost hidden by more overgrown shrubbery. It had a little sliding panel, which was closed, and underneath that there was a sign tacked up that read DUNGEON!

Emily gasped. "I had no idea we had a dungeon, did you?"

"That sign doesn't look very official," said Thomas, and he knocked briskly on the door. The children waited.

"I think maybe I heard something," whispered Emily after a few seconds. "Maybe some people scuffling around? I hope they're not mad!"

"Or *dead*," Thomas whispered back.

"Nobody's dead—we've already decided." Emily knocked on the door again. They waited. "I definitely heard something this time!" she whispered. "Like some people arguing but trying to be quiet about it." They put their ears to the door, and both clearly heard a woman's voice say, "*All right*. I guess I'll get it, as usual! Everyone keep quiet." Then they heard the noise of a chair softly scraping on the floor, followed by footsteps. The children looked at each other nervously.

"Yes?" said a loud, crabby voice as the little panel was abruptly jerked open. Two eyes appeared. They looked past them, then down. The eyebrows shot up in surprise.

"Who are you?" the eyes demanded.

Thomas cleared his throat. "Um . . . so . . . hi," he said. "My name is Thomas, and, uh, this is Emily, and . . . it's possible that we may have shot an arrow through your window there . . ."

"We certainly hope no one was killed or wounded," put in Emily helpfully.

"And if, uh, they were . . . it was totally an accident," Thomas continued. "And we'd like our arrow back."

"And is this really the dungeon?" asked Emily.

The eyes, which seemed to belong to a woman, regarded the children with new interest.

"This isn't exactly the dungeon," she said at last. "Just our little joke."

"Oh," Thomas said. "Well, how about our arrow, then? We're pretty sure it went through your window."

"I'm pretty sure it didn't," said the woman. Then she turned and yelled over her shoulder to some unseen occupants of the room. "Everyone pipe down! It's just some kids . . . Yeah, the little nobles, I think. Back to work!" She turned back and looked at the children again. "No arrow here!"

"Why don't you ask someone in there?" said Thomas.

"No one saw anything—trust me," said the woman. "They're far too busy working."

"Maybe they did see something," said Emily. "Maybe you should ask."

"Maybe I should just send you on your way and get back to all the extremely important things I was doing."

"Can't we come in and take a look around for ourselves?" asked Thomas.

"Absolutely not!" said the woman. "Can't have children in here . . . Far too dangerous. Way too many . . . I don't know—pointy things."

"We're not afraid of pointy things!" said Emily. "We're archers! Please, we really need our arrow. It's one of the good ones, and the archery master makes such a fuss when we lose any of them."

"You shouldn't go shooting them through windows,

then!" said the woman. Then she turned again and snapped, "Put that back! I *told* you: we're working through lunch!"

"What's going on in there?" asked Thomas.

"Nothing for you to worry about," said the woman. "Why don't you just run along, my little nobles? It's been lovely chatting and all, but really, it's time for us to get back to work. No arrow here." The panel snapped shut and the eyes were gone.

Emily pounded on the door. "Wait! You have to tell us what you're doing in there! Our parents own this castle and—"

The panel shot open again, and the eyes, narrowed now, looked down at them. "Oh, they do, do they? Look, kids, I know your mother from way, way back—I'm talking from when we were kids, before the dragon lived here, even—"

"DRAGON?" Thomas and Emily exclaimed at the same time.

"Here? A dragon lived *here*?" Emily squeaked.

"Yes, yes, of course a dragon lived here," said the woman, rolling her eyes. "Did you not know that? Frankly that surprises me, smart little nobles like yourselves, with your education and all, not knowing the history of your own castle. Fancy that. Kids today." Then she added, "You should ask your mother about it sometime. Like how about right now?" The panel closed again.

"We can't ask Mother—she's away at a conference with our father," said Thomas to the door.

"Oh, away at a conference? Oh, yes, your mother is so important. I've heard. Mm-hmm."

"You could tell us!" Emily pleaded.

The panel opened again, and again the eyes appeared, clearly exasperated. "Look, kids," the woman said. "I'd love to tell you the story, really I would, but this is not a good time, understand? We have a terrible deadline in here." And the little panel shut again, clearly for good this time.

"Well, how do you like that?" Emily said as she and Thomas walked back to their archery things. "What a strange person."

"Definitely strange," Thomas agreed. "And I don't think she's telling the truth. She says she knows our mother, but I've never heard Mother mention her."

"You're right! Why hasn't she been over for dinner and lawn games like Mommy and Daddy's other friends?"

"Definitely strange," Thomas repeated. "And also extremely crabby."

He looked up and groaned. "Oh, great, here's the archery master! Wait until he notices I lost our best arrow."

"We might find a way to get that arrow back," said Emily. "And maybe hear that lady's story, too!"

"I'd be happy with just the arrow," said Thomas.

Then both children ran to meet the archery master, who was standing exactly seventy-five paces away.

Chapter Two

I think we have to at least entertain the possibility that the lady in the basement is a witch," Thomas said to Emily later that day as they crossed the field back to the tower in the outer wall.

"Can you see Mommy letting a witch live in our castle? Really, now," said Emily, swinging a basket covered with a cheerfully embroidered cloth.

"Yes, but if they knew each other when they were little—and I'm not sure I believe they did, but if so—maybe that's why Mother lets her live in the castle now," Thomas said. Then he added thoughtfully, "And it's not necessarily bad for a castle to have a witch, you know. I met a kid at camp last summer who said they have a witch at *their* castle, and she was really good at making medicines out of roots and leaves and flowers and stuff. You know, for curing you of warts or whatever, not just for turning you into a newt. Frankly all the best castles have a witch, is what he said."

"Thomas, I *know* witches can be good. I just don't think that lady *is* one. I think she's just an . . . interesting lady."

"Well, witch or not, I hope she's in a better mood now than she was this morning," Thomas said.

"Me too!" said Emily. "I want her to tell us the story."

Thomas groaned. "Oh, please, it can't possibly be true! I mean, a dragon living here? Mother and Father never said anything about a dragon! I can't imagine them living in a castle that used to have a dragon in it!"

"Oh, I can't, either! That's why I need to hear the story," Emily said as they descended the stone stairs. She hid the basket behind her back and knocked politely on the door.

Again, there was muttering, the sound of a chair scraping on the floor, and muffled footsteps approaching. The little panel jerked open.

"You said we had until five!" said a voice irritably. Thomas and Emily were not surprised to see the same pair of eyes from the morning look past them . . . and then down.

"*False alarm!*" the woman called back to whoever else was

in the room. "Just the little pests again, the ones who think we have their arrow"—she turned back and glared down at the children—"which we absolutely *do not*. So don't even ask."

"Can we come in?" said Thomas.

"Of course not!"

"Well, will you come out, then?" asked Emily.

The eyes rolled. "You've got to be joking. We're so busy in here, I can't even tell you."

"Too busy to eat these?" said Emily as she produced the basket from behind her back. She whisked the cloth away with a flourish.

The woman's eyes widened just a bit. "What might you have there?"

"Oh, just some beautiful tarts right out of the oven, with raspberries Thomas and I picked ourselves after our morning lessons," said Emily nonchalantly. "Don't they smell just wonderful? We knew you'd be hungry, because you said you were all working through lunch . . ."

"Wait—this is some kind of trick, isn't it? What are they, poisoned?"

"We're just being nice!" said Emily. "All you have to do

is open the door and you can have them—the whole basket! They're toasty warm and really, really delicious. Thomas and I already had two each."

"Five," corrected Thomas.

"Thomas!"

"They're small!"

"How about just put them through the little window here, one by one?" said the woman.

"Emily is much too short to reach up that far," Thomas said. "Why not just open the door?"

"And have you both run in here and ransack the place? I think not," the woman said.

"We promise we won't," said Emily. "You can trust us!"

"Hmmmmm," said the woman, looking at the tarts longingly. Her eyes narrowed, and their corners crinkled into what the children perceived to be the ghost of a smile. "Oh, all right!" she said. The panel snapped shut. A moment later, the lock clicked, and the door scraped softly on the stone step as it slowly opened just a few inches. The woman peered out at them almost shyly from the dimness of the room, her face nearly hidden by the hood of her cloak. A grimy hand, smudged with black, extended from a sleeve so rumpled and stained, it was hard to tell what color the fabric was.

"All right, all right, door opened. Now hand over the grub."

Emily gave her the basket. "Are you serious? These are really for us, and they're good and tasty and not poisoned, not even a little?" the woman said incredulously. "I have to say this really is awfully kind of you little nobles! No one ever gives us nice things. Honestly I don't know what to say."

"Say you'll tell us the story," said Emily.

"And you'll give us the arrow," put in Thomas.

"And you'll tell us your name, so we can stop calling you that lady who lives in the basement," Emily added.

"Arrow no, name no, story yes," said the woman, "seeing as it looks like I won't get a minute's peace unless I tell you. But outside."

"Yes, yes, too dangerous in there—pointy things—we remember," said Emily.

"I was *going* to say," said the woman, "that maybe I *would* actually come outside for a little while. Let me give these out and get my coffee. Why don't you two go sit on the grass right there by the window? I can't go far. I have to keep an eye on things, you know. Can't leave these people alone for ten minutes—they'll probably burn the place down." She turned and quickly closed the door with a soft *fwump*. The children could still hear her grumbling through the door: "Not that I even have ten minutes. I have a million things to do, not that anybody cares, of course . . ."

The children climbed the stairs and went over to the grassy spot by the tower. Thomas flopped comfortably onto his back and put his hands behind his head. Emily took off her apron and neatly spread it out to sit on. She ran her fingers through the long grass, which was filled with little blue flowers.

"Look at these flowers, Thomas!" she said. "Aren't they pretty?"

"Flowers are boring," said Thomas with his eyes closed.

"I'm going to make a flower crown."

"Well, that will be doubly boring."

"I'll give one to the lady—she'll like that. It will help us make friends," said Emily, and she began to busily pull up flowers.

"Speaking of the lady, did you notice she wouldn't tell us her name, even when you asked?"

"Well, perhaps she thought we were being too forward," said Emily. "She *is* a grown-up, after all."

"Yeah, probably a grown-up *witch*," said Thomas, "who wouldn't tell us her name because it takes her witchly power away or something. I doubt she'll even come out. She'll just sit inside and put a spell on us through the window while she eats our tarts."

"She'll come out," said Emily with certainty as she wove the stems.

Presently the woman appeared, wrapped tightly in a dark, tattered cloak and carrying a small cloth bundle and an ancient-looking mug. She plopped herself down on the ground next to the children.

"Hello again, my pesty little friends," she said pleasantly. "I see you're still here." She placed the mug carefully in the grass and unwrapped the bundle, which held a large handful of the tarts. She spread the tarts out on the cloth, which was, the children noticed, rather inky-looking.

"Did you think we wouldn't be?" asked Emily.

"Oh, I may have been secretly hoping, because it's terrible that I'm even out here at all. Who knows what mischief they'll get up to," the woman said, gesturing toward the window behind the bushes. She shook off her hood, pushed her long hair behind her ears, closed her eyes, and leaned back, turning her face up to the afternoon sun. "All right, I admit it: it's awfully nice out here. It wouldn't kill me to get a little fresh air now and again."

"Don't you ever come outside?" asked Emily.

"Oh, sometimes," the woman said vaguely, then popped a tart into her mouth. "Oh, my goodness, these are really good!" she said, chomping loudly. "Here, you have some, too!"

"We already had several on our way over," said Emily politely, eyeing the inky cloth.

"Well, they are absolutely delicious!" said the woman, stuffing another into her mouth and taking a loud slurp of her coffee. "Hey," she said, suddenly suspicious. "You didn't steal these, did you?"

"No, we get to have them whenever we want. We were just going to have them after dinner anyway," said Thomas.

"Nice to be a little noble, I see! Okay, good. I would hate for you to get into trouble on my account," the woman said. "Mmmm, just one more."

Just then a voice called fearfully from the basement window. "Meg? Are you out there? You may want to, uh . . ."

"I'm *busy*, Reggie!" the woman shouted back toward the window. "I'll be done in ten minutes!" She turned back to the children. "Do you believe that? I'm out here for five seconds and they're already bothering me."

"So . . . uh . . . Meg," said Emily. "Perhaps you could tell us the story, about the dragon? But first, look, I made you a flower wreath. You can put it on if you'd like. I'm making one for me, too. I would make one for Thomas, but he thinks flowers are boring."

"They are," said Thomas.

"They most certainly are not boring," said Meg. "Especially these flowers here." She looked at the wreath closely. "Hmmm, nice work. You have clever fingers; I can tell."

"Thank you," said Emily, beaming.

Meg continued to study the flowers. "Where did you find these?"

"You're sitting on them!" said Emily. "How could you not notice? They're all over the place. Aren't they pretty?"

"Huh, so they are! Did you know these flowers really are very useful?"

Here Thomas nudged Emily with his foot and mouthed, "See?"

"What?" said Meg.

"Thomas thinks you're a witch," Emily explained.

"I see. Why, because I have a big nose? Like I haven't heard that before."

"I ... uh ... don't think you have a big nose," said Thomas quickly. "And you're probably not a witch ... I guess."

"Ha, I wish I was! Don't worry, though: if I was a witch, I certainly wouldn't eat children! I would keep you alive so you could bring me these tarts every day," Meg said jovially, then gobbled down another. She took one more sip of her coffee, placed the flower wreath on her head, and said, "So. It seems to me that you really, really want to hear this story."

"We do!" said Emily.

"Well, I'll do my best, but just warning you: it's pretty long, and there may be some slow parts. I know how kids today like everything to be nonstop excitement."

"We're okay with it not being nonstop excitement," said Emily.

"And as long as it's true, of course," said Thomas.

"And I won't be able to tell you the whole thing right now because I'm only going to be here ten minutes. I'm sure your mother would be happy to tell you the rest."

"Mommy isn't here this week," said Emily. "She's a very busy noblewoman. She goes away to conferences a lot."

"I see," said Meg. "Oh, yes, your mother, so important—how could I possibly forget! I guess I'd better get started!" She took a thoughtful sip of her coffee and began.

"So, your mother, the young Lady Catherine . . ."

"Aren't you going to start with 'Once upon a time'?" asked Emily. "That's how stories usually start."

"Emily, don't interrupt right off!" said Thomas. "Give her a few paragraphs, why don't you!" Then he said to Meg conspiratorially, "She interrupts *all* the time—you'll see."

"Well," said Meg, using the opportunity to delicately nibble yet another tart, "I didn't say 'Once upon a time' because this wasn't any old time, you see. It was a very specific time, when your mother was just a maiden, around sixteen or so. Plus, if I say 'Once upon a time,' you might think I'm telling you a fairy tale, and I'm not. This is a completely true story, with real people I actually know, like your mother."

"Okay," said Emily, "except that I really do like when stories start with 'Once upon a time.'"

"Well, if you want," Meg suggested, "you can imagine it's all nice and written out, with a lovely illuminated border, and the first letter in a box, maybe with a fantastical beast like a unicorn wrapped around it. Will that help?"

"Yes," said Emily. "I'm imagining it right now."

"Excellent. So your mother, when she was just a lass, lived out in the village there, the one we can see from the castle. She was out walking alone in the woods one summer day—"

"Mommy was in the woods *alone*?" said Emily. "We're not allowed to walk through the woods alone, *ever*!"

"That is generally a very good rule," said Meg. "There are all kinds of dangerous bears and wolves and weasels and even most likely gryphons. But remember your mother was a bit older than you, and sixteen, back in the old days, was pretty much grown up. And she would of course stay on the path, since she is so sensible."

"That sounds like you really do know our mother," said Thomas.

"Told you I did," said Meg, taking another sip of her coffee. "Your mother was on her way to the meadow to pick flowers—just like these little blue ones right here—even though they were right in front of the castle . . . the castle where the dragon lived!"

"Did people *know* there was a dragon?" asked Emily.

"Of course people knew! The dragon had been sighted many times. At sunset he'd fly back from the village, usually with something that he'd found in his claws—spoons or coins or shovels, even bicycles!"

"Why would a dragon want a bicycle?" said Emily.

"It's common knowledge that dragons love shiny things," said Thomas. "They are notorious treasure hoarders."

"Absolutely!" said Meg. "This dragon stole things from people's yards all the time, and people were really afraid of him. Still, your mother—even though she was, as we know, the most sensible person in the world—risked going near the castle to pick these little blue flowers. She needed them because she had to weave a tapestry for one of her damsel classes—"

"Ooh, tapestry weaving!" said Emily. "I'm learning how to do it, but Thomas won't."

"Tapestries are even more boring than flowers," said Thomas.

"I feel sorry for Thomas, then," said Meg. "Tapestry weaving is a wonderfully meditative pursuit, very helpful if you have a lot of thinking to do! And you know, back then, it was absolutely required knowledge for a well-brought-up young person. And before you could begin weaving, you had to spin the yarn yourself and dye it, and that meant making the dye. You couldn't just waltz into the yarn merchant and buy whatever fashionable color you wanted, as the young folk of today do," she said, looking meaningfully at Emily.

"I do prefer the more modern methods," said Emily, busy with her wreath, "as I'm sort of a more modern type of girl, you know."

"I see," said Meg. "Interesting you say that, because your mother, *once upon a time*, considered herself rather a modern girl, too—far too modern for old-fashioned fairy-tale beasts like dragons. And that's where her troubles began! People, including some very dear friends even, tried to tell her the dragon was real, but your mother, with all her book learning, thought she knew more than everyone else—"

"But she *does*," said Emily. "Doesn't she?"

"Maybe not that time," said Meg, taking another sip of coffee. "Anyway, if you pick lots and lots of these flowers and boil them in a pot, you can make the most heavenly blue dye, and that's the color your mother needed."

"Mommy really does like things just so," said Emily. "But still, I can't see her risking picking the flowers on the dragon's front lawn. That just sounds too adventurous. Mommy is more sort of . . ."

"Boring," said Thomas.

"I was going to say 'cautious,'" said Emily. "But maybe it was market day, and she thought the dragon was off doing its errands."

"Good theory," said Meg. "And possible. Like I said, your mother was very sensible. But there she was, so busy picking flowers that she didn't notice the giant shadow that glided over the field."

"*Finally* the dragon shows up!" said Thomas. "It's about time—there's been nothing but flower picking so far."

"Yes, it was the dragon!" said Meg. "He swooped down on his huge horrible bat wings and plucked your mother right up in his big, sharp horrible claws!"

"I bet it would be so fun to be picked up by a dragon!" said Thomas.

"You know that feeling where your stomach seems like it's jumping out of your mouth? That's probably what it felt like," said Meg.

"I love that feeling," said Thomas.

"I personally would not find it pleasant," said Meg. "Anyway, he carried her off and locked her in one of the castle towers—"

"*This* tower?" asked Emily, alarmed. "This one right here that we're sitting next to?"

"Oh, no, that would be too much of a coincidence," said Meg. "I think it was that one, over there. The one on the other side of the gatehouse."

"That is *so* mean!" said Emily.

"Well, duh!" said Thomas. "That's dragons for you.

That's why knights have to vanquish them! I intend to vanquish at least several someday, when I'm a knight."

"As if Mommy's going to let you be a knight," said Emily. She turned back to Meg and said, "I need to get a better picture of what's going on here. Like, what was Mommy wearing? Did she have one of those tall pointed hats with a veil on it? I *really* want to wear one of those hats, but Mommy won't ever let me. She says they're for fancy balls only, and we haven't had one for such a long time."

"Don't you know about the one coming up?" asked Meg. "It's going to be big—three hundred guests at least. Proclamations, invitations, menus . . ."

"No one tells us anything!" said Emily.

"Fancy the two of you not knowing about your own parents' anniversary party!" Meg said, then took another long sip of coffee.

"Their anniversary party?" said Emily. "Oh, how wonderful!"

"Yes, that's why it's so big. They're trying to invite everyone who came to their wedding all those years ago."

"Oh, our parents' wedding!" Emily said dreamily. "I've so often wondered about it! Was it fabulously romantic?"

"I have no idea. I wasn't there," Meg grumbled. "Look, do you want to hear the story or not? If you don't, I should probably get back inside."

"Yes, back to the story, please," said Thomas. "All Mother had to do was find a knight to vanquish the dragon, obviously. Any properly trained knight could do it."

"Easier said than done," said Meg. "Don't forget, your mother was completely alone, and no one saw the dragon take her away. No one even knew she was gone."

"Not even Grandmother?" said Emily, shocked.

"Nope, not even your grandmother," said Meg, breaking the last tart in half. "Your mother was actually away at college at the time, so her parents had no idea their only daughter had just been plucked off the face of the earth by a dragon and locked in a tower."

"Yes, but, if—" began Thomas.

His question was interrupted by a muffled crash from the basement, followed by a sort of despairing wail and various scuffling sounds. Meg jumped to her feet. "What's going on in there?" she shouted toward the bushes.

"Oh, nothing. Don't worry!" a voice answered, followed by whispers and the sound of broken glass being swept up.

Meg sighed. "Story over, kids. I have to get going anyway. So much to do, including dealing with whatever ridiculous thing just happened in there. If they spilled the ink again, I swear I will feed them to the gryphons!" This last part she shouted into the window.

"But you barely even got started!" Emily protested.

"Sorry, really! Nothing I can do about it."

"Can we come back tomorrow?" asked Thomas.

"Can't promise anything," said Meg as she hurried back to her door.

"What if we bring more treats?" said Emily.

"Wouldn't hurt! Goodbye, my little pests!" said Meg, and she disappeared back into the tower.

Chapter Three

he next afternoon, as the children again descended the stone steps of the outer tower, they were surprised to find Meg leaning against the door frame and whistling absentmindedly to herself.

"Oh, look, you're waiting for us!" said Emily, delighted. "I'm so glad we don't have to go through that whole knocking-on-the-door rigamarole again, with you having to act like you're mad at us and everything."

"Well, if it isn't my new friends, the little pests!" said Meg, very obviously pretending to be startled. "I wasn't actually waiting for you; I was waiting for . . . the mail. The mail coming is the highlight of my day."

"The mail came at eleven," Thomas pointed out. "Like it does every day. It's very reliable."

"Did it, now?" said Meg. "Imagine that. I guess we were so busy in there, I must've missed it. Maybe I just wanted some fresh air, like we got yesterday. It was really very enjoyable."

"Maybe you wanted to sit outside and tell us more of the story, and eat some nice lemon scones!" said Emily, whisking the cloth off her basket.

"Scones!" came a voice from inside, and a small cheer went up.

Meg rolled her eyes. "Do you see what I have to put up with? I absolutely cannot have a private conversation! They're always listening in. You can see why I'd want to come outside every now and then, wouldn't you?"

"Oh, please can't we come in, to meet the others?" pleaded Emily.

Meg sighed and shook her head. "I really don't think you want to go in there."

"We really do!" said Thomas and Emily at the same time. "If we don't get to come in," Emily added resolutely, "we'll take our scones and we won't come back! I didn't want to say that, but you leave us no choice."

"And you know, these are excellent scones," said Thomas. "I had three on our way over."

"Is that so! Oh, my goodness, you little nobles drive a hard bargain. I see I have met my match. You are mighty crafty and persistent. Good thing I like that in the smaller humans! All right, then, you have gained entry." Meg pushed the heavy wooden door open and gestured for the children to follow her. "Don't say I didn't warn you, though."

Thomas and Emily followed Meg timidly across the stone floor into the round basement room. It was cool and dimly lit from the one high window. Two men and two women in dark robes like Meg's sat at tall wooden desks arranged in a haphazard circle, pens in their hands, surrounded by all sorts of jars and bottles and ink pots, cups and plates, and a few lit candles, too. But mostly there was paper everywhere: in stacks and piles and rolls, and crumpled up into balls all over the stone floor as if many mistakes had been made. The men and women looked up at the children expectantly.

"Please . . . uh . . . excuse the mess," said Meg. "It's usually as neat as a pin in here. You know how it is: sometimes the housekeeping starts to go when you get really busy."

"Busy doing what?" asked Emily, fascinated by the sea of paper.

"Copying and illuminating, of course! Say hello to Lester, Myrta, Kitty, and Reggie . . . the castle scribing department!"

"So *that's* what goes on in here!" said Thomas. "We had no idea!"

"Nobody does," said Meg, and there were grumbled murmurs of "of course not" and nods from the men and women at the desks.

"Are they hungry?" Emily whispered to Meg. "Can I give them each a scone?"

Meg nodded solemnly. "I think they would all love a scone. Treats are the best way to become popular around here."

"Hooray! We knew they'd bring us food!" said the closest scribe, eagerly grabbing a scone from the basket.

"Oh, really now, Reggie! We had lunch not two hours ago!" said Meg.

"And are they going to help us?" asked another of the scribes hopefully.

"Help you what?" said Thomas.

"Don't be ridiculous, Myrta! They can't possibly help us! They're just children. Besides, you know how young folk today are with their education. None of them have decent penmanship anymore—"

"I do! I do!" Emily piped up. "I have very good writing skills! We practice with Mommy *hours* every night!"

"It's true," said Thomas. "We're both really great at writing, especially me! Everyone knows it's important for knights to have good penmanship."

"Is that so!" said Meg. "Goodness me! Well, just so you know, we have to concentrate very hard for a long time, copying the same things over and over and over. That might be too much for you, even with your excellent penmanship skills. No, I could never ask such a thing of such sweet children who have already done so much for us." She shook her head demurely. "In fact, now that you've had your little visit, you should probably be running along and leaving us to our boring, important grown-up work."

"Please don't make us leave! It looks so fun in here," said

Emily. "Look at all the paper and paints and things! Can we draw pictures, too? I love to draw. And so does Thomas, even though he says he doesn't."

"Unfortunately today is writing only," said Meg. "No drawing. And really, we would love to have you, but I'm just not sure you would have the patience."

"We will have the patience—we promise!" said Emily, clasping her hands beseechingly and fairly bouncing up and down. "Please?"

"Well . . . hmmm. I know you *are* persistent. And seeing as you're already in here," said Meg slowly, "and you really, really want to . . . I guess *maybe* you could give it a try. Just a try, though! I'm not promising anything."

"Yay!" said Emily.

"All right, then. There's some space there on the bench next to Lester for Thomas, and you sit there, Emily—Myrta is making a spot. Have you both used these kinds of pens before? Good, good. You can just share the ink, and let me get you some paper." When things were pushed aside and the children were comfortably settled at their places, Meg continued: "All you have to do is copy exactly what these invitations say. Here's one for each of you that someone else already wrote out. Just write yours exactly the same way, okay? I'm sure such clever children will have no trouble."

"Oooh . . . these are lemon scones!" said Myrta. "You know what would go really well on these?"

"Don't say it," said Meg. "No one's going anywhere."

"What would go really well on them?" asked Emily, who couldn't help herself.

"Gooseberry sauce!" said Myrta, and all the scribes sighed longingly.

"Yes, yes, gooseberry sauce," said Meg. "Well, we don't have any, so why don't you all get back to what you were doing, and watch the crumbs, please. And, yes, children, these scones are beautiful, and perfect as they are, and we thank you—"

"Do gooseberries grow in the castle garden?" said Emily. "We could go get some!"

"They only grow in the forest," said Reggie. "So sweet and tart at the same time . . ." Again there were great sighs of longing.

"Thomas, look! This is the invitation for the big party coming up!" exclaimed Emily, waving it at her brother.

"Yes, yes, the big anniversary party," said Meg, rolling

her eyes. "It's all I've heard about for something like a whole year now. So extremely exciting. It's the night your parents come home from their trip, which is soon. Meaning the invitations have to be mailed out soon, meaning we actually have to finish them soon, meaning we all need to be writing them out right now!"

"I could run and pick some gooseberries really quick . . ." said Reggie.

"Will you *stop* about the gooseberries!" said Meg. "We have *way* too much work to spare anyone. Even you, Reggie."

"Hey!" said Reggie.

"Back to work," said Meg.

"Aw, come on, Meg!" Reggie pleaded. "The gooseberry patch isn't even all that far. It's just off the path where it splits from the road! I'll be back in twenty minutes!"

"You were gone for three hours last time, and we had to send the apprentice off to find you and then he got lost! Wait a minute: we found him, too, didn't we?"

There was a silence for a minute or two, then Myrta said, "Oh, yeah, remember we saw him the next day?"

"He was mad," added Kitty. "No wonder he hasn't been back!"

"I wasn't even lost," said Reggie. "I got the berries right away, but then I saw a gryphon a little way off and—"

"Oh, you didn't," said Meg.

"I did so! He was coming at me, so I—"

"Reggie, you absolutely did not see a gryphon."

"I did! I see them all the time! They're no trouble really. All you do is—"

"Is the party a surprise?" Emily asked, interrupting, as she examined the invitation. "Oh, I've been waiting *forever* for a fancy-dress ball to wear my new gown at! Grandmother made it for me. It's the most beautiful color—fuchsia, Mommy said it was. It's so pretty: it has short puffed sleeves and a shirred yoke and ribbon trim. The only problem will be my shoes, but—"

"I found a spelling mistake," reported Thomas, who had already started writing.

"Oh, Reggie, not again! I told you to check your spelling!"

"It wasn't me! Why do you always think it's me?"

"Meg, can you tell us the story while we're writing?" asked Emily, who had also started scratching away.

"Oh, yes! A story, Meg!" said some of the others.

"Meg often tells us stories while we're working, to keep

our spirits up during times of great difficulty," Myrta whispered to Emily, "of which there are many."

"All right, all right. I'll start, but if it looks like production is going down, that will be the end of storytime," said Meg sternly, sitting down at her table and fussing with her own writing things.

"Is this the story of that time you found a troll out back?" asked Myrta.

"Or the time the vampire followed you home?" said Kitty.

"Neither!" said Meg. "It's a new story—well, an old story, actually—about how a dragon used to live here—"

"*A dragon used to live here?*" shrieked Myrta.

Meg sighed. "Yes. A dragon lived here back when we were all just kids." She turned to Thomas and Emily and whispered, "Don't mind Myrta—she isn't from around here."

"You can't just start in the middle," said Lester.

Meg sighed again. "All right, all right. Yesterday I told the kids that when their mother was a young lass, the dragon who lived here, who was not very nice, picked her up right off the ground and locked her in one of the towers. Not this tower—another one."

"That was much faster than yesterday," said Thomas. "You didn't need all that about flowers and such."

"Details are very important," said Meg with a sniff. "You'll see. Now, is everyone all set with their invitations? We're all working? Okay, good. So Catherine—she was a friend of mine from the neighborhood when we were kids— we lived on the same street, played on the same tennis team, all of that stuff—was locked up in one of the high towers, frightened and alone."

"Was she crying?" asked Emily.

"I bet she wasn't," said Thomas. "Mother is pretty brave. There was a spider in the privy once and Father—"

"You can be brave and crying at the same time," said Meg. She put her pen down and leaned back in her chair. "I'd be crying if it was me! Just think how scary it would be to be all alone in the quiet dark of the dragon's cold stone tower with only one small candle for light."

Emily's pen stopped scratching. "I'm getting kind of sad thinking about Mother all alone in the dark in the scary tower."

"Well, don't worry: it wasn't sad for long! Because, all of a sudden, out of nowhere: *whump!* Something flew through the bars on the window and whacked her right on the side of her head!"

"Was it a rock?" asked Myrta, alarmed. "Are you sure you should be telling the children this?"

"Mommy was alone in the dark and got hit in the head by a rock?" said Emily, her voice trembling.

"No, no, of course not! It wasn't a rock. It was an onion! It flew right in the window and didn't even hit her head really. It hit her in the hat—you know, the tall pointy hat with the bit of veil on it—and knocked it right off her head! Your mother couldn't believe it. She called out into the night, 'Hey! Who did that?'

"Catherine didn't see anything, because it was already nearly dark. But she thought she heard some very faint laughter. At first she wasn't sure, because there are so many noises in the night, you know: the breeze rustling the leaves on the trees in the courtyard, the chirping of the little frogs, the hooting of the owls, the twittering of the swifts. But there was definitely the sound of laughter, too! It was soft, but she knew she heard it.

"'Who's there?' she called out.

"And a very small voice said, 'Oh, excuse us, miss!'

"Catherine peered down into the darkness. 'I cannot see you. Show yourself!' she called.

"'I'm right here, miss,' said the little voice. 'Out here in the grass.'

"'Where?'

"'Right here!'

"And it was then that Catherine knew she was being visited by the wee forest folk."

"Was it a fairy with wings?" Emily exclaimed, clapping joyously.

"Emily, you practically spilled your ink," Thomas groused. "Watch it, will you?" He turned to Meg. "You said

47

this wasn't going to be a fairy tale! Now there's a fairy in it."

"I never said it was a fairy," said Meg. "I said it was one of the wee forest folk, of which there are many different kinds, which you would know if you were getting a decent education, which I am starting to seriously doubt. Anyway, it wasn't a fairy; it was one of the little elves you see in the woods around here at night. And good thing it was an elf, because they are generally helpful and nice, unlike fairies, who can be a bit unpredictable. Or pixies! Those are the ones you really have to watch out for. They can be quite wicked."

"How did Mommy know it was a nice elf and not a bad pixie?"

"Well, pixies are very noisy, you know—they make all sorts of knockings, sometimes very soft and sometimes quite loud. This elf was quiet; your mother had barely heard the laughter at all. Also, pixies dress in bright colors and are especially fond of red hats, but elves dress in the colors of the forest, in woodsy browns and greens and shadowy grays. This elf was standing in the grass, and in those days, before your uncles mowed the lawns, there were a lot more of those tangled bushes and vines, so he blended right in."

"He sounds so adorable!" said Emily. "Was he very tiny?"

"Well, elves are small . . . smaller than you, but not nearly as small as fairies," said Meg. "Remember, this one had to be big enough to throw an onion."

At this, there was only the thoughtful sound of pens scratching away industriously for a few moments. Then Emily asked, "But *why* did the elf throw an onion at Mommy's head?"

"Right, the onion! Well, there was a whole bunch of these little elves running around the castle grounds that evening, and they thought the dragon was up there in the tower room, because they saw the candlelight. They decided to throw onions at him to vex him! Everyone knows dragons hate onions."

"Sometimes there are vegetables missing from the castle garden," said Emily. "We always thought it was rabbits."

"Nope! Elves," said Meg.

"Or us," said Kitty, "if we're working late and we really need some salad."

"I've finished an invitation!" Thomas announced.

"Ooh, let me see!" said Meg. "Hand it over. I say, very nice work! You really do have excellent penmanship! Look at this, Kitty," said Meg. "Pretty good, eh? Indistinguishable from Lester's."

"Oh, yes, and much better than the apprentice's," agreed Kitty. "That kid's work was awful. Full of smudges and fingerprints. This one is so much neater."

"I'm almost done, too," said Emily. "I would've finished before Thomas, but I dropped my pen and it took forever to find it with all the papers on the floor."

"It's not a race," said Meg. "And from here it looks like you have very nice penmanship, too. Thank you, Thomas. Put it over in that stack with Reggie's. And yes, just start another—plenty of paper. And good catch on the spelling mistakes. All right, everyone all set for now? I'll continue.

"Your mother explained her predicament to the little elf and asked if he could help find a knight to rescue her, and he said he would. The elves didn't like the dragon much at all, you know—he was always trying to eat them. Don't worry, Emily, he could never catch them! Elves run fast and are good at hiding. Most people think elves are very mischievous, and, of course, they are, but they are also generally good and kindhearted."

"Don't you have to offer elves your firstborn child or something?" asked Kitty.

"Hmm, now that you mention it, I think she may have had to do just that," said Meg. "But they weren't going to come take him until he was . . . oh, twelve or so . . . on midsummer's night. Wait a minute—what day is it?"

"Ha-ha, very funny," said Thomas.

"I'm kidding, of course," Meg said. "We all know it's fairies who do that. But back to our little elf, whose name was Acorn. Catherine asked if the elves could write out a notice and hang it on the message board in the village for a knight to see, and he said they would. So she fished around in her pocket and found a pencil and some candy wrappers—"

"Mommy never lets us have candy!" said Emily. "And she was just carrying it around? So unfair!"

"You will have to take that up with your grandmother," said Meg. "And please remember that your mother was a good deal older than you at the time, as I've said. She took the wrappers and wrote out what she wanted the proclamation to say."

"I'll bet Mommy had to eat a bunch of the candy first to get the wrappers," Emily said to Thomas, who nodded in agreement.

"So, yes, first Catherine had to eat the candy, then she wrote out what the sign should say on the wrappers, then she tossed them down to Acorn. He told your mother he would do his best, bade her good evening, and slipped off into the darkness with the rest of the elves."

"No knight is going to look at a message in pencil on a bunch of candy wrappers," said Thomas. "It wouldn't seem very professional."

"No, it wouldn't!" said Meg. "The elves had to write out their own proper proclamation to hang up. First they picked a bunch of blackberries from the dragon's garden . . . but then they ate them, so they had to go back and get more.

Those, they squashed into ink. Then they snuck into the town square in the dead of night—that's when all elvish business gets done, you know—tore down another proclamation, and wrote on the back of it with the ink. I don't remember exactly what it said, but we've done a lot of proclamations, and they generally start with 'Be It Known Throughout the Land . . .'"

"It's standard business procedure to offer the dragon's treasure in exchange for a rescue," said Thomas. "Because usually a knight would have to slay the dragon to rescue the damsel, freeing up the treasure and all."

"That sounds reasonable," said Meg. "Probably something along the lines of 'Be It Known Throughout the Land, a Fair Damsel Seeks Immediate Rescue from the Dragon's Tower, blah blah blah, usual terms apply, et cetera.' Then they tacked up their proclamation and crept out of town, back into the forest."

"What about the hand-in-marriage thing?" asked Lester. "Doesn't the knight who slays the dragon get the damsel's hand in marriage or something?"

"Ha, I can't see Mother going for that *ever*," said Thomas.

"Wait a minute—Daddy was a knight!" said Emily. "Is this also the story about how Mommy and Daddy met? He was the one who slew the dragon and then they got married?"

"Oh, yes, that's it, end of story! Aren't you smart! Wow, that was easy," said Meg. "How many invitations have you each done—four, five? Very nice! Why don't you both just finish up the one you're doing. I would hate to make you little nobles late for dinner."

"I absolutely cannot believe that Mother and Father meeting would have anything to do with a dragon," said Thomas. "Knowing them, it was at a stuffy conference about moldy old books and scrolls and manuscripts written in languages no one speaks anymore. They're really not the adventurous types. Although it *is* true that Father was a knight."

"There must be more to the story," said Emily. "We'll be back again tomorrow so you can tell us what really happened. Will there still be invitations to write out?"

"Most likely," said Meg.

"Good," said Emily. She picked up her pen again, and throughout the stone room, the only sound was of pens scratching thoughtfully.

Chapter Four

he next morning, as the sun was rising, the children, each with a willow basket, set off down the dirt road that led through the meadow in front of the castle.

"Look how sparkly everything looks! It's like there are diamonds everywhere!" said Emily.

"It's just the dew." Thomas yawned. "I can't believe you're skipping already, Emily! It's too early for skipping!"

"I don't think it ever is," Emily sang merrily as she skipped into the woods. "Won't the scribes be surprised? This is going to be so much fun."

Thomas yawned again. "Oh, sure, berry picking first thing in the morning. Most exciting thing ever." But he kept trudging after her. The sun was peeking through the trees that arched gracefully over the path, softly filling the woods with a misty, golden light. The children's footsteps made no sound on the soft pine needles. All they could hear were birds.

"I know Meg says the elves are out late at night, but do you think they're out early in the morning, too?" said Emily.

"Emily, there are no elves. Meg is just making them up for the story. And would you *please* stop skipping? It's so annoying!"

"I don't know why you believe in dragons but not elves."

"Well, obviously that's different."

"Look at all these ferns! Aren't they pretty and soft-looking, like feathers? I'll bet fairies live under them!" said Emily. "And then the very tiniest would live under these mushrooms—"

"Emily, stop! Here are the gooseberries already, just like Reggie said."

Both children crouched down and began to pick.

"You're crowding me!" Thomas complained. "These are my bushes—you go pick the ones a little farther up."

"But there's plenty here!"

"I like these bushes, and I saw them first!"

"Hmph," muttered Emily as she moved up the path.

"There's way more berries here anyway. And nicer ones, too." Both children picked in silence, their fingers flying.

After a few minutes, with her basket nearly full, Emily stopped and looked back at Thomas. "Did you hear that rustling?"

"Probably a squirrel. As you know, we are in the forest, home to many animals, including squirrels."

"Reggie said there are gryphons here."

"I highly doubt it, but even if there were, he said it's easy to frighten off a gryphon."

"Maybe it's one of the forest folk—and not one of the nice ones!" Emily turned around to look back into the woods. "Didn't that sound like . . . a knocking? What if it's pixies?" She looked back at Thomas, her eyes wide.

"Oh, my goodness gracious, Emily, do you really think so? Oh, dear me!" said Thomas.

"Don't make fun of me!"

"I'm not, I'm not . . . I'm sorry. Hey, wait a minute, I heard it, too . . . kind of a tapping . . . coming from over there!" He paused, listening. "There it is again!"

"You did hear it! It was a little knocking sound, right?"

"I did! It's true, just like Meg said!"

Tap-tap-tap.

"We should go!" Emily squeaked.

"Let's not panic! Where are the noises coming from? From the way we came or from the woods? Emily, you go look over there . . ."

With his sister turned away, Thomas quietly crept up behind her. Then he reached out and tapped two rocks together, right behind her head:

Tap-tap-tap!

Emily screamed and shot off like an arrow.

"Emily! Look over there . . . What's . . . what's that? Oh, my goodness, is it a *red hat*?"

Thomas sat down on his heels and had a long laugh. When he composed himself, he shouted into the empty trees, "Emily, that was me! I was just having fun with you! Come back!"

But she didn't come back.

Thomas rolled his eyes and sighed, then stood up. He started down the path that led deeper into the woods, breaking into a slow, loping run. "Emily, where are you? I was just teasing! I'm sorry, okay?" he shouted, and when he heard nothing in reply, he quickened his pace.

Emily was a fast runner, and she had had a good head start. The footing was uneven, and there were rocks and tree roots hidden under the pine needles as the path twisted through the trees before climbing up to follow a ridge. Thomas heard nothing but his own breathing, which was labored from the climb and from what he began to realize was fear. Was that finally a flash of her pink dress? He raced ahead, determined to not let her slip away. "Emily, *stop*! I was just—*aaaaah*!"

He felt himself skidding down a steep slope covered in wet leaves, and the next thing he knew, he ran into something hard buried in the leaves and went flying.

"Oof!" he said as he landed flat on his back.

"Thomas! Are you all right?" With great relief, he saw that Emily was there, crawling over to him where he lay. It looked like she had toppled down the hill as well. There were leaves in her hair, and her apron was all twisted around.

"The pixies, Thomas! They were right behind us! Come on, get up! We have to keep going!" she said, tugging urgently at his arm.

Thomas started laughing again. "You should've heard yourself scream!"

"What?"

"I was just knocking rocks together when you weren't looking! If you could've only seen yourself! You were terrified! I laughed for like half an hour."

"I *knew* you were just making fun of me!" Emily picked up a handful of leaves and angrily threw them in his face.

"Hey, cut it out. I . . . I think I actually hurt my foot. Hold on a minute. I tripped on a tree stump or something."

"You're just faking!" said Emily, throwing more leaves.

"No, I'm not. Look at my ankle: it's all scraped," he said.

"It serves you right," Emily said as she got up, shook the leaves off, straightened her apron, and walked back to see what he had tripped over.

"It hurts a little," said Thomas. "Not a lot."

"You didn't trip on a stump. You ran into this rusty old pole." Emily kicked through the leaves. "Funny that there's a metal post here in the middle of nowhere. And look! There's another one over there . . . and another one farther down. Is it an old fence or something?"

"Seems like a strange place for a fence, in the middle of

the woods. Though actually," Thomas said, looking around him for the first time, "this whole place seems a little strange, doesn't it?"

They saw now that they were on the edge of a great rectangular clearing, which was ringed on three sides by the slopes that led back up to the path. The side opposite them opened up to the forest, mostly thin young trees at first, and one very large oak that spread out over the clearing.

A look of amazement slowly spread over Emily's face. "Thomas! This is an old tennis court!"

"That's just silly. Why would there be a tennis court in the middle of the woods?"

"Didn't you hear Meg say something about how she and Mommy used to be on the same tennis team? It was right before she started the story yesterday."

"I was concentrating on my writing."

"She said they used to play tennis, and it really is a tennis court! Two of them, actually, right next to each other!"

"Enough already! You know Meg's just making the whole thing up!"

"No, you really have to look at this!" Emily had fully uncovered the metal post, which had been hidden by years of dead leaves piled up all around it. It may have once been painted green, and there was a metal ring at the top, with a bit of old rope tied around it. "This is one of the posts that held a net, and then there's another one there, and then another set! And look, Thomas." She came back and crouched next to him, scooping away handfuls of dead leaves. "The ground underneath is all packed down hard. It's a tennis court! What else could it possibly be?"

Thomas shrugged, then sighed. "I can think of no other explanation."

Emily's voice dropped to a whisper: "And over there on the other side, through the trees . . . Does that look like a little house to you?"

Thomas followed her gaze to the dark shape set back a little way into the trees. "It might just be a big rock—hard to tell," he said. "I don't know who would be living out here alone in the middle of the woods besides witches or trolls or maybe some nutty old wizard. We should get going."

"Yeah, we should go get our berries before the elves do," said Emily.

"Or the pixies," added Thomas with a smile.

Emily untied her apron and wrapped it around her brother's ankle.

"I promise not to skip," she told Thomas as she helped him to his feet.

"Thanks," he said, and together they scrambled back up the hill.

"I told Emily you'd only let us back in if we brought food," said Thomas, handing Meg a bag of scones. They'd also brought the berries, which Emily was hiding behind her back.

"Did you, now?" said Meg, clearly pleased with that idea and also with the scones. "Aren't you a perceptive lad!"

"Is that true?" asked Emily.

"Of course not," said Meg, "now that I know what good little junior scribes you are. But if you ever happen to sprain your hand, well, then you might want to bring in something especially tasty."

"Like a whole cake," called out Reggie from his desk.

"With giant flowers made out of frosting," added Myrta. "That's our favorite!"

"I have told you *so* many times—we can't ever have frosting here!" said Meg. "It gets on the paper. And you all get too crazy."

"Giant cake, no frosting," Myrta said with a sigh.

"Well, we did bring something especially tasty. Look— gooseberries!" said Emily, bringing forth the willow basket. A cheer went up from the scribes.

"Aren't you wonderful!" said Myrta.

"These kids are the best apprentices *ever!*" said Kitty. "That other kid, what's-his-name, never brought us any- thing good."

"In fact, he was the opposite," said Reggie. "He ate my lunch once! He said it was an accident, but—"

"And we didn't just find the berries. We found some tennis courts, too!" said Emily.

"Imagine that! Well, you must've gone a bit farther than the gooseberry patch," said Meg.

"Emily thought she heard pixies," Thomas explained. "She just ran off."

"She definitely may have heard some pixies!" said Meg. "The woods are thick with them. So you really found the tennis courts?"

"What was the instructor's name there . . . Krankybumpken?" said Kitty.

"Krackengully," said Meg. "He used to live right next to the tennis courts, in a funny little house all covered with moss."

"We saw the little house! I think there was smoke coming out of the chimney! But Thomas was afraid a wizard or a troll lived there, so we left."

"I wasn't!" said Thomas. "It was more like I knew Emily was nervous and I didn't want her to feel bad, because she was already so scared of the pixies, so I was just pretending to be scared, for her sake."

"Huh, old Krackengully is probably still there. Fancy that!" said Meg.

"So Mommy really played tennis with you in the woods?" Emily asked.

"Oh, yes, we were always on the same team. We were partners forever! One year we went all the way to the Tri-Village Tournament."

"You did? Was Mommy good at tennis?" asked Emily. "She's never talked about it!"

"She was okay, but I was better," said Meg with a sniff. "She probably doesn't talk about it because she feels bad she never showed up at the tournament that day, but I got the last laugh. I won the whole thing myself!"

"Oh, please! You did not," said Reggie. "I was there that year, too, and—"

"Did so," said Meg. "Krackengully wanted me to pair up with that Kenny kid from down the street, but I was too mad. I said no, thanks, I'll play alone! Won the doubles all by myself, I did! But enough about tennis." She walked back to her desk and picked up a pen. "Now, I have some good news and some bad news. The good news is that you kids did an excellent job with the invitations yesterday! The bad news is that I met with Lord Gabriel, the castle party planner, and he thinks they're not quite ornate enough for the royal party, so we have to pretty them up a little. He thinks everything has to have great swooping scrolls and swirly decorations. Nothing's ever fancy enough for him!" Meg dipped her pen into Emily's inkwell and drew a quick flourish at the top of an invitation.

"I also thought they weren't quite fancy enough," said Emily. "I mean, it's going to be a very grown-up party with a huge dinner and many, many cakes and dancing and everyone wearing their best clothes! I myself will be wearing my new fuchsia gown. It has flowers embroidered on the collar—"

"Oh, I like that idea, a little flower, with some scrolly stuff. That looks nice," said Meg, adding one.

"It looks like the blue flowers from the other day!" said Emily.

"So it does," said Meg. "Would you like to draw some, then?"

"Of course I would!"

"I don't have to draw flowers, do I?" said Thomas. "Personally I would rather keep writing. It's more serious than decorating."

"Excellent—you're very good at it," said Meg, sitting down in her own chair. She leaned back and put her hands behind her head. "And I will do what I'm good at, which is telling this story. Let's see, where were we? Oh, yes, the elves made their own proclamation on the back of someone else's proclamation—"

"You know, I was a little worried about that," said Emily. "What if the proclamation the elves took down was important, like for a lost kitten or something? Did they even think about that?"

"Well, here's the funny thing about elves," said Meg. "As

I said before, they do have kind hearts and can be helpful at times, but they don't always think about the consequences of their actions. And also I'm not one hundred percent sure that elves can read, though they pretend they can. I would think if the proclamation was about a lost kitten, though, there would be a picture of one."

"Don't worry, Emily," said Reggie. "I actually saw the proclamation around here when we were cleaning once. It was just an advertisement for Blodgett the privy digger. Don't worry about him; he has lots of business. He did all the castle's."

"See? No harm done," said Meg.

"All right, then," said Emily. "Keep going!"

"After the elves hung their proclamation, they slipped out of town and ran back through the woods and met at the base of Catherine's tower to report on their progress."

"How did the elves get to Mommy's tower at night? The drawbridge is only down during the day," said Emily. "Except when we know someone is coming in the middle of the night, like when our uncles are coming in late from travels then it gets put down specially."

"Emily, think of it!" said Thomas, exasperated. "The

elves wouldn't go over the drawbridge—the dragon would definitely know!"

"Yes, Thomas is quite right: the elves would never go over the drawbridge," said Mcg. "When they break into the castle grounds, as they so often do, they swim across the moat, avoiding all crocodiles—"

"But they couldn't do that at night!" said Emily. "And why do elves get to swim in the moat and we don't?"

"Sometimes we swim in the moat at night!" said Kitty. "In the summer, when it's really hot. That's one of the reasons we like it out here."

"Our mother would never let us swim in the moat at night, ever! Especially if she thought there were crocodiles."

"We've never seen one," said Myrta. "But Reggie has!"

"Reggie's crocodile is a story for another day," said Meg. "I don't want us to get sidetracked. Especially when it's *not true*."

"Is so," Reggie muttered. "Unlike some of *your* stories, like last week when you said you saw a troll wearing my new hat—"

"And he looked quite dashing in it," said Meg. "Anyway, where were we? Oh, yes, crocodiles. There probably used to be crocodiles in the moat, though nowadays I really doubt it. But the elves have their ways to avoid being eaten by both crocodiles and dragons, who are distantly related, of course! When they get into the moat, they swim really fast, and then they sneak through this little secret tunnel that goes through the wall and comes out into the swimming pool—"

"What swimming pool? We don't have a swimming pool!" said Thomas.

"A lot you know! You didn't even know about the tennis courts!" Meg scoffed. "There's an old swimming pool out behind the garden, and the elves swim through and help themselves to vegetables and berries whenever they want. Very convenient."

"Not that it's really a swimming pool that humans would use," Reggie added. "Trust me; we've tried. It's kind of murky, with lots of frogs and turtles. Even worse than the moat."

"They met at the bottom of the tower," Meg continued, "and told Catherine that help was on the way. Then, since it was a beautiful night and the moon was full and high up in the sky, they took out their flutes and drums and other elvish instruments and played their sweet mysterious music to keep her spirits up. Elves love to do such things, you know: play music and dance at night, out under the moon. They do it all summer long. That's another good thing about working here, late at night—we hear them sometimes, far off, out in the woods."

"I would love to hear them! We love music, too! I'm learning the flute, and Thomas takes lute lessons. In fact he has to go to his lute lesson right before lunch, so we can only stay a little while today."

"Well, I'm glad to hear you two are finally learning something useful in your education. Maybe you could play for us sometime, when things get especially dreary."

"Like when we have a million invitations to do," grumbled Lester.

Meg continued. "The next morning, knights on their steeds began to ride out of the woods and assemble on the grass next to the moat, near the drawbridge. It had been an effective proclamation: there were at least fifty of them there by lunchtime! Such a splendid sight: the knights all in their shiny armor, their magnificent steeds in their . . . their little blankets—what do you call them?"

"Surcoats," said Thomas.

"Yes, surcoats! Also imagine all the knights with their lances and swords and spears, and their shields, which of course all bore their various heraldic devices. You know, their individual identifying designs. Stripes and symbols and such, in their special colors. Very important."

"Absolutely!" said Thomas. "My heraldic device is going to be a mighty lion, with some chevrons and whatnot. I can't wait."

"Mighty lion!" Myrta giggled. "Sweet little lion cub, more like it."

"The day stretched into the afternoon, and it grew hot. The flies came, and that bothered the horses and made them restless, and that made the knights restless, too. At three o'clock, it seemed time to start. But the drawbridge was up, and of course they had to get in somehow."

"The proper way to get into a dragon's castle," said Thomas, "is by shouting 'Dragon! Grant Us That We Mayest Access Thine Terrible Lair!' You have to use the old-fashioned words—that's what makes dragons pay attention. They are ancient creatures who don't go in for modern talk, you know."

"An authority!" said Meg approvingly.

"Well, I know all this stuff from my knight lessons," said Thomas, shrugging but looking pleased. "You have to know all the details about the things you have to fight."

"The knights shouted out what Thomas said they would've, and then slowly, inch by inch, the drawbridge began to lower."

"Was the dragon lowering the drawbridge?" asked Emily.

"Emily, that would be ridiculous!" said Thomas. "That makes no sense at all! If the dragon was lowering the drawbridge and standing there while the knights rode in, how silly would that be? He could just roast them as they went by— that wouldn't be sporting at all! There are rules, you know!"

"Even a dragon has standards," Meg agreed. "And what if the dragon let them in but immediately had to run after them and get into fighting position?"

"Awkward!" said Thomas.

"Yes, not at all dignified for such an ancient creature," said Meg.

"Plus everyone knows he has to rise majestically from the keep," said Thomas.

"You know how nowadays old Oskar lifts and lowers the bridge?" said Meg. "Back then, the dragon had to have a helper to do that, and a bunch of other things, too! Think of all the things he couldn't do around the house with those big wings and that tail bumping into everything, not to mention those big clumsy claws! He couldn't wash the good dishes or weed the garden. His helper was a young forest troll—I think his name was Jerry. He was very nice. You couldn't really blame him, working for the dragon—hard for a troll to get work in those days. So as I said, the drawbridge slowly lowered: *click, click, click.* Then faster: *click-click-clickclickclick, whomp!* The drawbridge hit the ground, and the castle was open for business."

Just then the story was interrupted with a pounding *bang-bang-bang-BANG!* on the door.

"Oh, great," said Meg. "Didn't you kids say you had to run along to your music lessons?"

"Why, who's at the door?" asked Thomas.

"Oh. No one. Just, uh . . ."

"*Meg!* Are you guys done in there? How many more left?" an unseen man's voice bellowed.

"Just a second!"

"It's Lord Gabriel!" Myrta whispered to the children. "The invitations were supposed to be done today, and they're not."

"Gotta go, kids," said Meg. "Out, out with you!"

"Just when it was getting good," said Emily.

"Here, climb out the window," said Kitty, getting up from her seat. She pushed a small table against the wall. "We do it all the time. Meg doesn't want Lord Gabriel to think we're in here having nice company and eating scones and gooseberries and not writing out invitations."

"Why can't we just go out the other door, the one that leads out into the hall?" asked Thomas.

"One of the guards might see you. Don't you think it's more fun to go out the window? We do!"

"Well, wouldn't he be happy we're helping?" asked Emily as she climbed up onto the table.

"Not sure," said Kitty. "And we don't want to find out! Thanks for coming today. You guys are really good helpers! Out you go!"

Chapter Five

t was raining a little the next morning as the children walked through the wet grass to the tower.

"I hope they don't throw us out the window again today," said Emily.

"That was the best thing that's happened so far," said Thomas. "Well, besides finding the tennis courts. I guess that was okay, too."

"I think helping with the writing and the drawing is also fun," said Emily. "And you can tell that Meg really appreciates us coming by."

"Of course Meg likes us helping. Haven't you noticed she doesn't work very hard when she's telling the story?" said Thomas. "Not that I would ever say that; I prefer not being turned into a newt."

"Meg is *not* a witch! And did you ever think, maybe telling a story is hard work?"

"Oh, sure, if you have to make it up as you go along, which is what Meg is obviously doing."

"But can't you see that everything is true so far? The tennis courts are real!"

"Right, and if *they're* real, then there *must* be elves and pixies," said Thomas sarcastically.

"Shh!" said Emily. "We're here!" She poked her head in the door. "Hello, hello! We don't have to knock anymore, do we?"

"Of course not. You work here now for real!" said Meg, who was not at her usual place but standing underneath the window, in front of a large white board on a wooden frame. "But you're here a little early today, no? Isn't this your skullduggery lesson time?"

"*Archery*," corrected Thomas. "And it's canceled, because, in case you didn't notice, it's raining. On the one hand I hate it when archery is canceled, but on the other hand it's okay, because the archery master hasn't noticed yet that we lost our best arrow. Not that I'm, you know, looking for it or anything."

"Good," said Meg, "because it's still not here. And of course we always notice when it rains! That's why there's a jolly little fire going in the fireplace, and all these extra candles are lit. Please be extra careful not to knock anything over today; there have been incidents. I mean, if you still want to help, that is! Or did you only want to bring us that lovely basket full of delicious-looking something-or-others?"

"That would be okay, too!" said Myrta, helping herself to what was in the basket, which was an assortment of tiny muffins, all different flavors.

"But just a teensy bit less okay than helping," Meg added.

"What are you doing, Meg?" asked Emily as she passed out muffins to the happy scribes.

"It's another brilliant idea from Lord Gabriel." Meg sighed. "It's going to be a big painting of your parents as they looked on their wedding day. Do you know how much work it is to make the paint? First, you have to go into the basement and find all the rocks, then you have to grind them— "

"That is *so romantic* and lovely!" said Emily. "A picture of Daddy and Mommy in their wedding clothes! I know you're only drawing it out rough now, but is that really what her dress looked like?"

"I have no idea—I wasn't there," Meg said. "But your grandmother found the dress up in the castle attic for me. I'll do the best I can with it, but, good grief, it's just a dress. No one will remember it exactly. It's okay if it isn't perfect."

"And was her headpiece really . . . a big hat?"

"Again, I have no idea. Your grandmother couldn't find the headpiece, so I just thought of something myself. Why, don't you like it?"

"Well, it's okay, I guess. It's just that you can't really see her eyes too well, or her hair."

Just then there was a sort of muffled, thumping knock on the door that led from the hallway, and an enormous box seemed to clumsily push its way in.

"Well, if it isn't my good friend Lady Dara!" said Meg. "Bringing us something wonderful, I'm sure."

The children saw then that the box was carried by a very short woman, who slammed the box down on top of Reggie's table.

"Let me guess," said Meg. "We're making every guest a special fancy party hat with their name on it in sparkly letters?"

Dara laughed as she opened the box and pulled out a handful of envelopes. "No, no, I don't think we have time for that! The big boss decided he doesn't want the invitations scrolled. We're going to fold them and stuff them. Envelopes have so much more class and timeless elegance, he says, whatever that means!"

"I think it means more work for us, as usual!" said Meg.

As Dara pulled out the envelopes and started stacking them on the table, she noticed the children for the first time. "Why, hello there, young miss and young master! Fresh young faces! New apprentices already? You never found the others?" she asked Meg.

"They're not official apprentices really," said Meg. "More like, oh, temporary help. Kids, meet Lady Dara, assistant to Lord Gabriel. This is Thomas and Emily, the little nobles from the castle."

"They can be from the moat for all Lord Gabriel could care, as long as they're quick!" said Dara.

"Quick as little bunnies, they are," said Meg proudly.

"And can they fold?" asked Dara.

"I don't know—we don't really fold much in regular life," said Thomas, who did not appreciate being called a bunny.

"That's not true, Thomas!" Emily piped up. "Don't you

remember when Mommy showed us how to make birds out of paper? They weren't cut at all, only folded."

"I wasn't there. I was probably off doing important knight training."

"You were so there! You made one out of purple paper. How can you forget? Mine was blue. And we decorated them and everything, and then we made some little tiny baby ones, and then nests out of grass clippings, and we said they lived on Bird Street, and then we pretended—"

"I have absolutely no memory of this."

"Thomas doesn't want you all to think he still plays with paper birds."

"I *don't!*"

"You'll have to show them the folding, Dara," said Meg. "I have charcoal all over my fingers at the moment."

"In half, just like this," said Dara. "Easy enough for two very clever children. Make sure they're nice and straight!"

"I'll be much better at this than Thomas," said Emily.

"No way!" said Thomas. "Look, I've already done three and Emily's barely started."

"No squabbling, now—this isn't a contest," said Meg.

"It could be, though!" said Lady Dara. "Let's see which

one of you can do more! My money's on the little miss—anyone who can fold a bird can fold an invitation! Here, I'll sit and fold some, too."

"I also like to fold paper dolls," said Emily.

"I love paper dolls!" said Myrta. "We could make some together sometime. We have this nice heavy paper, and then whenever we have leftover bits, I save it. We could use it for the clothes, and—"

"Not until this job is over! Focus!" said Meg. "Meanwhile, I will keep telling the story. Now, where were we?"

"We're at the part with the knights!" said Thomas. "They're on their steeds, waiting at the drawbridge."

"Right! The elves were there, too. They were very interested in the goings-on. They were a little nervous, though, and didn't want to get too close, so they were all sitting in the big beech tree that's right out in front of the castle, in the meadow there. And of course Catherine was also watching from her window. I'm not sure how the knights decided who was going to cross over the drawbridge first, but one did—Sir Monty, I think it was."

"It's a great honor to go first!" said Thomas. "Because if you're the first one over and you vanquish the dragon right off, you get the treasure and that's that and you can brag about it forever. It would be the best!"

"Don't you think you'd have a better chance if you waited more toward the end, when the dragon was more tired?" asked Emily.

"Maybe, but everyone knows it's more *honorable* to be first," said Thomas.

"I'm sure Sir Monty thought so, as he bravely clopped over on his magnificent steed, his lance held high and his shield—which bore the heraldic design of two stripes and the silhouette of a camelopard—glinting in the sun. The elves watched Sir Monty cross the bridge into the darkness of the gatehouse, and then reappear in the sunlight of the courtyard. Then he turned and galloped to the left, out of their view. The dragon then indeed rose majestically from the keep, just like Thomas said—and terrible and majestic he was! The elves heard the slow, heavy beats of his huge bat wings as he descended into the courtyard. They couldn't see him because he was right under your mother's tower, but they could see smoke rising over the wall! Then the hoofbeats started as Sir Monty and his steed began their charge. Clop! Clop-clop! Clop-clop-clop!" Meg left her drawing and clopped her hands on Emily's table.

"Sorry to interrupt the dramatics," broke in Dara, "but I see some crooked invitations! It's important that they be nice and straight!"

"Yes, around here you have to be able to hear a dramatic story *and* keep folding straight at the same time," said Meg sternly, walking back to her canvas. "You have no idea how picky Lord Gabriel gets about these things."

"Meg is terrified Lord Gabriel will yell at her again, like yesterday!" Kitty said with a giggle.

"Oh, he didn't!" said Dara. "I will have to talk to him about that."

"He didn't really," said Meg. "All right, where was I?"

"Clopping! You know, clop-clop, clop-clop-clop!" said Emily.

"Ah, yes, impending mayhem!" said Meg. "The elves watched Sir Monty's steed gallop full speed toward the dragon. Sir Monty leaned forward, his lance raised, ready to strike! They couldn't see what happened next, but there was a terrible crashing noise, and then a terrible gnashing-of-teeth noise, and then growling and roaring and other terrible dragonish sounds. Then clop-clop-clop-clop! Sir Monty and his horse came racing back out over the bridge!"

"He retreated?" asked Thomas, looking up from his folding, shocked. "I can't believe it! How cowardly!"

"Have you ever *seen* a dragon, much less one blowing flames at you?" said Meg, pointing her charcoal at him. "Don't be too quick to judge poor Sir Monty! I'm not sure he had ever really seen a dragon, either. That's probably why he was so blithely eager to go first! Next up was Sir Ramone, I think, though I could be mistaken—I'm only going by what I heard. Anyway, not that it matters, as he, too, came clopping right back out, and listen to this! His horse's tail was on fire!"

"Oh, my goodness!" said Emily.

"Yes, his steed risked being eaten by crocodiles by jumping into the moat to put the flames out!

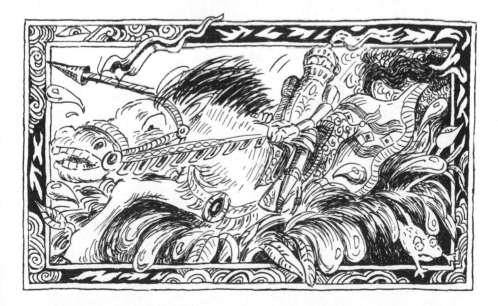

"You'd think that would dissuade the rest of the knights, but no! They just kept lining up and clopping over, one by one. One by one the dragon took them on. Most came galloping back, the horses looking a little singed, a crazed look in their eyes. Some of the knights just went crashing through the woods back to town, while others dismounted and sat on the ground, moping dejectedly and refusing to talk about what they had seen. Still, knights kept lining up, one after the other, clopping over that bridge, some all pumped up and cocky, others more timid and hesitant."

Emily raised her hand, as if she were in school.

"You there with the yellow braids, yes?" said Meg.

"Just a suggestion. Why didn't the knights all gang up on the dragon instead of going over one by one? I would think they'd have a better chance that way."

"That isn't how it's done!" said Thomas. "Everyone knows the knight slays the dragon and rescues the damsel to prove his valor, and he has to show he can do it alone!"

"But wouldn't it make more sense? I mean, clearly it wasn't going well."

"I totally agree with you, Emily!" said Meg. "You are a sensible girl, just like your mother! If they only wanted to slay the dragon, maybe they would have joined forces, but don't forget, each knight also wanted the dragon's treasure all to himself! They didn't want to share it."

"Knights," said Dara, wearily shaking her head in dismay. "You know how they are."

"I don't think they were necessarily greedy," said Thomas. "I think it's more that they wanted it to be a test to prove their individual valor."

"Perhaps," said Meg. "For whatever ill-advised reason, the knights kept dispatching themselves, one by one. They clopped over; they ran back. Until they started to not come back at all! The first to not come back was Sir Bartholomew, and he had an especially sturdy steed, Neal."

"Are you saying the dragon *ate* them?" asked Emily.

Meg nodded solemnly. "Probably, though no one saw it happen. They never came back out. I'm afraid we must assume the worst."

"This story is much more horrible than I thought it would be. I didn't think horses would get eaten!" said Emily.

"You can't have a story about a dragon where no one gets eaten, Emily!" said Thomas.

"I'm afraid the boy's right," said Meg, turning back to her artwork.

"The story may have taken a turn for the worse," said Dara, "but we have some good news! We're nearly done with the folding! And was I right? I think the little miss has a slightly taller stack of folded invitations."

"Mine are folded tighter, so they take up less space," said Thomas. "More finely crafted."

"Here's the last little bit of story I'm going to tell you, because I have to go down and start making my paint," said Meg. "After the last six knights failed to return, the rest of the knights and their steeds slunk back to the woods to make their camp for the night. They were demoralized and filled with a sense of foreboding. Which means they had an anxious feeling that something bad was going to happen."

"We knew what it meant," said Emily.

"I said it more for the benefit of Reggie."

"I knew what it meant, too!"

"I've got a sense of foreboding as well," said Dara. She held up a folded invitation for Meg to see. "What do you think Lord Gabriel will say about this?"

"*Not fancy enough! Too plain! This is a fancy party!*" bellowed Meg in a gruff voice, and Dara laughed.

"Should we draw a few flowers on the front, like the one on the inside?" asked Emily.

"Ugh, more boring flowers," said Thomas. "Can I just draw scrolly stuff? It's more serious."

"I like these kids," said Dara.

"Me too," said Meg.

Chapter Six

on't you think it's odd that Mommy and Meg used to be friends but they're not anymore?" said Emily as she and Thomas walked through the courtyard on their way to the tower room. "It sounds like they haven't talked to each other in years! And Meg is telling the story from the point of view of the elves, not Mommy. I noticed that right off."

"Oh, you also saw that her only sources for the story are mythological creatures? I think that only proves that this story is one hundred percent made-up silly nonsense, and Mother will most likely say the same thing when she gets home."

"And Meg's told us a bunch of times that she didn't go to the wedding! Mommy definitely would've invited all her friends, so that means either they *weren't* friends or Meg just didn't go!"

"And *that* would've really made Mother angry! She's a stickler for stuff like that."

"Maybe Meg is still really upset about that tennis tournament . . . you know, Mommy not showing up and her having to play all by herself. Maybe she got really mad about it, refused to go to the wedding, and is still mad, even after all these years."

"Well, I'm sure Mother had a good reason not to show up. This is *our mother* we're talking about! I don't know why Meg would be so mad anyway. What's the big deal? I would love the chance to play a doubles tournament by myself! It would be an excellent chance to show off my skills. I mean, if I knew how to play tennis. I'm sure I would be good at it. It's probably sort of like jousting or something."

Emily ignored her brother and continued: "I just think it's so terrible, being best friends with someone and then not being friends with them anymore, over something so silly! Here they are in the same castle, and they never even talk!"

"Are you sure Meg even lives in the castle?" said Thomas. "I mean, if she's a witch, she probably lives in a hollow tree in the woods and comes in here for her day job as a scribe."

"Oh, stop," said Emily.

They were at the tower steps now. The heavy wooden door was propped open, and Meg was busily painting by the window.

"No one likes the paint fumes," explained Meg, who seemed quite pleased that the children were there, bearing a large basket of little cinnamon rolls. The scribes all had enormous stacks of envelopes in front of them.

"We skipped our geography lesson to come help!" said Emily. "We know the invitations have to go out today! We said the cauliflower pie gave us stomachaches, but it really didn't."

"You skipped your lessons just for us?" said Meg. "I—I don't know what to say! I think I'm going to cry!"

"In the whole history of the world, this has never happened," said Myrta.

"This is a very special day," said Lester.

"And speaking of this being a very special day, we need to be done by three o'clock, which is in barely two hours!" said Meg. "Dara brought us the list of addresses straight from Lord Gabriel himself, and we've been writing them out all morning, but there's still quite a few to go. They're being delivered this afternoon. The party is Saturday, and it's already Tuesday!"

"It doesn't seem like all that big an emergency to me," said Thomas. "Emily insisted."

"A party coming up fast *is* an emergency!" said Emily. "Everyone has to get their invitations in time so they can get their outfits ready! I mean, I know I'm going to wear my fuchsia gown, but I still need to decide what to wear over it. Should I wear my best lace pinafore or perhaps my smartest little jacket? I like the jacket, but I'm not sure the color will go. Usually Mommy helps me pick my special outfits, but she isn't here now, so I have to decide myself. And then there's the question of shoes . . ."

"Not everyone needs four days to pick out their clothes, Emily! Be like Father and me: pants, shirt, boots—*done*!"

"I hear some *do* enjoy wearing special clothes to events they are actually happy about attending," said Meg. "But enough about dresses. Let's talk about *add*resses! Myrta will show you the ones we've already done. Make sure you use your most extra best, most special handwriting. People love seeing their names all written out nicely. And absolutely no spelling mistakes! Not that you would do that, of course—clever little well-educated children that you are, even with missing your geography lesson!"

Papers and inkpots were pushed aside, and the children settled into their regular spots. Emily scanned the list of party guests. "I see all my aunts and uncles and cousins!" she said. "This will be so fun! Oh, great, Cousin Penelope is invited. Oh, I bet *she'll* get to wear a hat with a veil on it!"

"She's eleven," Thomas explained to the others. "Emily is only nine."

"Practically everyone from the castle is invited," said Emily. "But what about the cook? Shouldn't she get to go?"

"Everyone who works at the castle is automatically invited. We just don't bother with invitations for ourselves," said Meg. "As for everyone else, they have to be on the official party guest list provided to us by Lord Gabriel, no exceptions. We do take our job pretty seriously! Not that you'd think that sometimes."

"Oh! You're all going to the party, then!" said Emily with great delight.

"Of course!" said Myrta. "We love parties! The food, the dancing . . ."

"And speaking of dancing," said Emily, "I'll be doing a dance with all my friends from class! We're all going to be in a long row, and we'll each have a different color dress. It will be like a rainbow! I'm in fuchsia, of course. Olina will be in green, then Suki is in yellow. At first Roseanne wanted to be in yellow, but we all decided—"

"As interesting as that sounds," said Meg. "I'd rather not."

"You have to go!" said Emily. "Parties are the best! You get to dress up and—"

"I hate dressing up," grumbled Meg, turning back to her painting.

"But you have to go!"

"Are you kidding me? I've heard about nothing but this party for weeks now—I am thoroughly sick of it! Plus, I have to get moving on the next project, the heraldry for the junior jousting team, if I ever finish this confounded painting, of course."

"The painting! I forgot to look at how it's coming along!" said Emily, leaning back in her chair to see. "It looks so nice! Oh, my goodness, look at Mommy with long hair! I'm glad you took that awful hat off. I'll try and find her headpiece— I'm sure it was pretty. But . . . hmmmm . . ."

"Now what?" said Meg crossly.

"Oh, just . . . her bouquet. Was it really toadwort?"

"Well, again, I have no idea what her actual bouquet was, so I just went with some favorite flowers of mine. Why, not good enough?"

"Not exactly the prettiest flowers I've ever seen."

"They have many medicinal qualities."

"But that isn't always what you want in a wedding bouquet," said Emily.

"First the hat, now the flowers," Meg muttered. "And I suppose you'll want your story now, to add to my troubles."

"Yes, please," said Thomas. "You were at a good part about the dragon. If it's not too much bother, of course."

"Right, the dragon," said Meg. "It was evening, and the knights had had such a terrible day with him. They were becoming flustered and filled with a sense of foreboding— you know, from their fights and since some didn't come back at all."

"Presumably devoured!" said Thomas, who found this part particularly fascinating.

"But not definitely?" said Emily hopefully.

"Probably," said Meg, growing more cheerful.

"Sorry, kid!" put in Lester. "Tough world, hungry drag-ons and all."

"I don't think they really got eaten," Myrta whispered comfortingly to Emily. "They were probably just hiding back in the garden."

"Myrta has no idea what happened," said Meg. "But I do! That's why I'm the one telling this story. As I was say-ing, things were not going very well for the knights. There was an uneasy feeling in their camp at the edge of the woods that evening. Oh, sure, there was still talk around the camp-fires of them going in for battle the next day, but it was less enthusiastic, let's say. The elves, quietly hidden in the trees, eavesdropped of course, and occasionally stole a marshmal-low or two from the knights' fires. They sensed the knights' courage was faltering, so a little group of them decided to visit Catherine to discuss what to do. They swam the moat, slipped under the wall through their secret tunnel, got out of the pool, snuck through the courtyard, and climbed up the tower to Catherine's window."

"I'll bet Mother didn't approve of them climbing up the tower at night," said Thomas, very familiar with these matters.

"Probably not," said Meg, "but she understood that these

were desperate times. And of course, elves can do whatever they want—your mother wasn't *their* mother! Four or five elves climbed up, Acorn among them. They sat on the windowsill and talked with your mother, and they all came up with a plan to ambush the dragon."

"Ooh!" said Thomas.

"Yes," said Meg. "So the next day, three elves—Acorn, his little brother Robin, and Bonnie—"

"Finally a girl elf!" said Emily.

"There have been girl elves all along. I just haven't mentioned any of their names yet," said Meg. "The three of them hid under some bushes on the path right outside the village, just before it goes into the forest. It was a little sunny spot where the mail carrier would stop and build a fire and have his morning tea and a nap on the days he went to the dragon's castle. Elves pretty much know everyone's business, all the comings and goings through the forest. It's not that they're nosy exactly—more just curious about everything. They like to keep an eye on things."

"Was it our mail carrier, Mr. Connolly?" asked Emily.

"Emily, this was like fifty years ago, when Mother was

a girl!" said Thomas. "Mr. Connolly wasn't even born yet probably."

"Ahem," said Meg sternly. "First of all, this was *not* fifty years ago! Not even half that! And mail carriers do tend to have remarkably long careers thanks to all that fresh air and exercise. So maybe it was Mr. Connolly and maybe it wasn't, but whoever it was, he had his tea and then stretched out next to his cart and his donkey, and went to sleep in the morning sun, as he so often did. This is when the elves put their plan into action. They crept up very quietly and rifled through his mailbag and picked out three large envelopes. Then they carefully put the kettle back over the fire, which was still burning, and steamed each letter open."

"Does that really work?" asked Thomas skeptically.

"Of course!" said Reggie. "Not that we've ever tried," he added quickly.

"After the elves opened the letters, Bonnie and Acorn helped Robin into one of the envelopes, because he was the littlest and needed the most help. They sealed him back up as carefully as they could, and got him into the mailbag. Then Bonnie put an envelope over Acorn's head and sealed him up and got him into the bag, too. Then she had to get into an envelope herself and seal it up while she was inside, which was difficult, but she did it!

"And then she also got into the bag. And so when Mr. Connolly or whoever it was woke up, he had no idea there were three stowaways in his mailbag! And if his donkey knew—"

"What was the donkey's name?" asked Emily.

"Pomegranate," said Meg after a second.

"Probably not a necessary detail for the plot," Thomas remarked.

"No, but I don't mind!" said Meg cheerily. "So the mailman and Pomegranate—"

"Did he call her Pommy for short?" asked Emily. "I would."

"Now I am actually starting to mind the interruptions," said Meg. "And I have no idea. They bustled on through the woods as usual, coming out onto the path through the meadow that leads up to the moat. By now the knights were beginning to assemble on the grass, just as they had done the day before. You could tell they were looking at the whole drawbridge area with a very distrustful attitude. Not one of them made a move when the bridge came down, as it did around eleven or thereabouts on the days the mail carrier came. Unlike the knights, he didn't have to yell anything to be let in. Jerry would watch for him, let down the bridge, and he and Pomegranate would clop over. The portcullis wouldn't be raised, though. The mail carrier would just push the mail in through the bars, then turn and go back, and Jerry would raise the bridge back up."

"Didn't the mailman notice some of the mail moving?" asked Emily.

"Maybe he thought it was one of those new meal-delivery services!" said Thomas. "Like the dragon ordered a bunch of rabbits for dessert after eating knights all day!"

"Thomas, that is *gross*," said Emily.

"It's just an idea," said Thomas.

"Not a bad one," said Meg, considering it thoughtfully. "But the elves were trying very hard to impersonate mail by not wriggling, so I don't think he could tell. Bonnie and Acorn went right through the portcullis. Robin, though, well, he was a plump little fellow. The mailman pushed and pushed but he couldn't quite get him through, and I think maybe Robin didn't really like being pushed through the bars and started squirming. Whatever happened, Robin didn't make it through the portcullis with the others. Somehow he fell out of the mailman's hands and rolled off the drawbridge and splashed into the moat!"

"And the mailman didn't notice?" asked Emily.

"I don't think so," said Meg. "Or if he did, he didn't do anything about it."

"That seals it—it definitely wasn't Mr. Connolly. He would *never* drop mail into the moat and pretend not to see it," said Thomas. "He's very professional."

"Yes, well, apparently standards were a little lower back then," said Meg.

"It's true," said Kitty. "I remember not getting the mail for a whole week once when I was a kid. The mail carrier claimed a goblin stole her mailbag, which makes absolutely no sense, if you think about it."

"And once I sent away for a real gryphon feather pen, and I never even got it!" said Reggie. "Eventually I just made one myself."

"Oh, right, your rooster feather pen!" said Kitty.

"It's a gryphon feather!"

"I've finished my last address!" Emily announced.

"I only have one left, but I had more names on my list than Emily," said Thomas.

"Excellent!" said Meg. "And then I was hoping to find two strong young volunteers to help me carry all these invitations to the mailroom."

"Oh, take us! We want to see it!" said Emily.

"I was hoping you would," said Meg.

"The new kids get to have all the fun," complained Reggie, "going to the mailroom and such."

"You can help the kids get them all organized," said Meg. "Every time I let one of you guys go to the mailroom, I start thinking you've fallen into the moat, since it takes you so long to get back!"

Once the mail was arranged, the children followed Meg out the back door and onto the landing. They began to climb up the steps that led to the main corridor. Behind them, stairs spiraled down into darkness.

"What's down that way?" asked Thomas.

"Oh, just our storeroom, where we send the apprentices to go look for things when we find them tiresome," said Meg cheerfully as they climbed. "Sometimes they don't come back."

"You don't find us tiresome, do you?" asked Emily.

"Oh, not yet," said Meg. "There's still time, though!"

They left the darkness of the basement behind and turned down the corridor of the outer wall. It was much brighter here, with light streaming through tall, thin windows cut into the thick stone.

"We almost never get to walk here," Emily whispered.

"Mother doesn't want us to bother the guards. She says they're very busy guarding."

"There aren't very many guards here in these peaceful times," said Meg. "Usually just a few in the guardroom up ahead. Not much for them to do these days—I think they mostly play cribbage. Don't tell your mother; she wouldn't like that, I'm sure."

"Castle guards are always vigilant," said Thomas.

"Some of the time, I suppose," said Meg as they walked quickly down the long hallway.

"Ooh, look—there's a guard at the end!" said Emily. "With a long pointy spiky thing."

"That's called a pike, Emily!" said Thomas. "You're supposed to know your armaments!"

"Yes, a guard in action, properly guarding the guard-room—would you look at that," Meg murmured to the children. She stopped in front of him.

"Afternoon, Meg!" the guard said, tipping his helmet. "Lovely day, is it not?"

"It is, indeed!"

"Children," said the guard, giving them a nod. Thomas nodded back, and Emily dropped into an elegant and formal curtsy.

"May I present the noble children, Thomas and Emily. Children, please make the acquaintance of our celebrated and faithful captain, the most honorable, steadfast, and true guardian of your castle."

"Oh, Meg, how you do go on. Passage is permitted!" said the guard, blushing slightly. He thumped his pike on the stone floor and stepped aside. Meg pushed the door open. As they passed through the guardroom, four or five guards snapped to attention so quickly that their playing cards went flying. Meg nodded to each of them as she walked through, then, on the other side of the door, said "I never remember that guy's name. It might be Charlie, but I'm not sure. That's why I give him a very grand title—he never notices. It also helps when I can't think of the secret password. They make such a fuss when you can't remember, like it's a big deal or something."

They were in the gatehouse now, the space between the drawbridge and the castle's outer wall. It housed the portcullis, the big iron gate that blocked the entrance to the castle, and all the machinery—heavy pulleys, chains, counterweights, and gears—required to lift both it and the drawbridge. Since it was daytime, the drawbridge was down.

"Shouldn't the portcullis be up?" asked Emily, holding on to the bars and gazing through them into the meadow in front of the castle.

"It should be. Perhaps old Oskar is slipping," said Meg. "Didn't you see him in the guardroom, playing cribbage with the guards? He'll be raising it soon enough, like as soon as we get these invitations to Theodore!"

"So the mail carrier who was not Mr. Connolly put the elves through here?" Emily asked.

"Yes. As you can see, the spaces between the bars are definitely wide enough to put some dragon-size mail through, even mail with elves in it! And Jerry started pulling the drawbridge right up after the mail cart crossed back. The elves suspected their window of time was small. What if, after Jerry raised the drawbridge, he took the mail right to the dragon and opened it for him?"

"Because the dragon couldn't open mail with his big claws!" said Emily.

"Right! They knew they had to get out of there fast. So when he turned, like this, to crank the drawbridge back up with this big gear thingy here—"

Just then, the door opposite the guardroom opened and a man's voice said sharply, "Hey, Meg, how about instead of playing with the drawbridge you get me those invitations you were supposed to give me yesterday? You know Theodore's waiting for them! He'll be here any second now. What's this? Being head scribe not keeping you busy enough these days? You're a governess now, too?"

"I wasn't playing. I was—oh, never mind. And I'm *not* governessing, Frederico. These are my two very talented friends who've been helping out in the scribing room."

"A little young to be apprentices, don't you think? Well,

it *is* hard to find good help nowadays. What happened to that other one, by the way? Did you ever get him out of the well?"

"We're not actually official apprentices," said Emily.

"Wait a minute. You're the little nobles, aren't you! Dara told me," Frederico said as he stepped out of his room into the gatehouse. "She said you kids are pretty good, better than all the other apprentices put together, even!"

"Not that that's saying much, but, yes," said Meg.

"Well, isn't that nice! Anyway, no time for chitchat. Theodore's got to deliver these invitations all in one day. He'll be riding all over the place. I have to get them all in order."

"We did that already!" said Thomas. "This bag here is for the ones that go to town, and we put them in order by street and put strings around them so they wouldn't get mixed up with the ones that have to go into the countryside. Those are in Emily's bag."

"My, that's impressive! Hey, these kids really are good, aren't they? Maybe they'll even replace you, Meg!"

"Ha. I'd love it. It's my master plan. I can't wait, actually."

They were interrupted by cries of "Comin' through! Comin' through!" A man on a great silvery horse rode into the gatehouse from the courtyard side. The horse's hooves rang on the smooth stones of the gatehouse floor as he skidded to a halt. "Are my invitations here? Where's old Oskar? Let's get this portcullis raised!"

"Thanks, guys," said Frederico as he took the bags and began stuffing the envelopes into the horse's various saddlebags. "Hey, Oskar!" he yelled. "Put down the cards and get out here now! Theodore's ready to go!"

"Have a good trip, Van Nelson!" said Meg, giving the horse an affectionate pat on the nose.

"See you at the party, Meg?" said Theodore.

"I doubt it."

Emily sighed, then said, "Back to the scribe room now?"

"Nah, what do you say we keep going?"

"Really?" asked Thomas.

"Yes, really," said Meg as they passed through the mailroom, which was filled with all sorts of envelopes, scrolls, and interesting boxes and parcels, mostly wrapped in string and brown paper. "Since we're out, and since you obviously don't know a whole lot about the outside part of the castle here, I was thinking maybe I would take you on a little tour of the tower where your mother was held prisoner. I can keep telling you the story, too—if you don't have somewhere else you have to be, of course! I know you already missed some of your extremely important lessons. Hmmm, what did you have this afternoon, advanced rapscallionery? Or intermediary ciphering?"

"We know you're just making fun of us," said Emily. "But we don't mind. And we'd love to see Mommy's tower!"

They left the mailroom and entered another corridor,

similar to the last one, quiet and illuminated by the same tall thin windows.

"Sometimes I walk out here all the way around the outside wall when I need a break from the bunch of them," said Meg. "Especially when they're driving me batty, which is pretty much every day."

"Really? I think they're nice!" said Emily. "Myrta and I are going to make paper dolls, and did you know Kitty also plays the flute? She said we can try to play duets sometime. Thomas said he might play, too, on his lute, which would make it a trio! I've been asking him all year if we could play together, but of course he only wants to do it if a grown-up is involved—it can't be *just me.*"

"And Reggie said we could go crocodile hunting with him next time he goes," added Thomas.

"Again with the crocodiles!" said Meg. "The nonsense they fill your noble little heads with! I doubt your mother would approve of croc hunting, knowing how she is."

They came to the next tower and paused for a moment at the stairs, which wound all the way up and also descended into the darkness of another basement room.

"Are there more scribes down there?" asked Emily.

"That's actually the real dungeon," said Meg. "It's where all the apprentices who make spelling mistakes and fold things upside down and spill the ink go."

"You're just kidding, right?" said Emily.

"We'll just have to see what happens if Lord Gabriel finds a spelling mistake," said Meg. "I think Reggie had to go down there for a whole week once! But for now, we'll just go up."

"Race you, Thomas!" said Emily, and the children thundered up the steps.

"I'll just follow along in a manner more befitting the dignity of my age and position," Meg called after them.

Chapter Seven

he children reached the top of the landing first and sat down on the top stair to wait for Meg to huff and puff her way up to them.

"I always forget just how tall these towers are," she complained through her huffing.

The stairs ended in front of a heavy wooden door with iron hinges, but there was a little space at the landing for a small chair and table. Meg sat down in the chair. "I'm just going to sit and catch my breath," she said, "and then I'll tell you a little more."

"Are you sure the others won't mind that we're hearing more of the story than them? I don't want them to be upset," said Emily.

"You are one thoughtful young lady! Don't worry—I'll

fill them in later. There's still lots of work to do when I get back! Now that all the invitations are out, we have to start on the menus. First I have to meet with Lord Gabriel and the cook, though—"

"The elves started running after they got dumped through the portcullis with the mail," Emily prompted.

"Right! The two remaining elves, Acorn and Bonnie, in their disguises, ran toward your mother's tower. They scurried through the mailroom—not that it was a mailroom then, mind you—then down the hall and up this long, long winding stair. Can you imagine how hard that must've been, running in an envelope, up all those stairs with their short legs, hardly being able to see anything? Bumping into each other, bumping into the wall. It's a wonder they didn't tumble all the way back down! But they made it up.

"Now, Catherine had told the elves that the dragon brought her lunch up at noon every day. The mail came around eleven, and it probably took them fifteen minutes or so to get up here, so they had a little bit of time before the dragon came. They crawled underneath this little table I'm sitting at and pushed themselves right up against the wall. They were counting on the fact that it was dark up here, and also that dragons don't see very well. Usually elves aren't too afraid of dragons, but that's in the forest, where they can run and know the best hiding places and where they blend in really well. It was a lot different being in this dark place, in the dragon's own house, so out of their natural element! Nothing to do but huddle in fear and wait for the sound they dreaded most. The sound of the dragon—slowly, very slowly—climbing the tower stairs! Think of it: his heavy thudding feet, the *click-click-click*ing of his claws, his long tail dragging behind him . . ."

"The dragon draggin'!" Emily giggled.

"Sure, it sounds funny to you now," said Meg. "But imagine being squashed under this tiny table in an envelope! You would hear his claws and his scales and his big armored plates scraping along the wall, and I don't know, his big bat wings rubbing against the stones. I've never personally heard it myself, but I can imagine it's a horrible sound! And don't forget, the dragon was holding a tray, so he had to be extra careful, and it probably took him forever to get up here. He couldn't just run up, like you spry noble youngsters.

"The elves heard the dragon place the tray on the table above them, then he turned and went to open the door with his keys. Now, these were regular human-size keys, and the dragon of course has very long claws—that's why he had to put the tray down on the table to manage. With the dragon turned away, Acorn and Bonnie rocked the table together. Catherine had told them the dragon always put a flower in a tall pewter vase on the tray, and the elves thought if they knocked it over, the dragon would surely bend over to pick it up . . . because any dragon fussy enough to have a flower on his tray would surely pick it up, right?"

"This is preposterous," said Thomas. "Why on earth would a dragon put a flower on a tray? No one would do that, and—and he's a *dragon*!"

"Well, I think the dragon wasn't really used to having prisoners, and he was trying to do a good job," said Meg. "All in all he was a very good cook. He always made nice soup, with fine homemade bread, and even treats sometimes."

"When I have my own castle someday, and I have prisoners in the dungeon, I will feed them only bread and water, like you're supposed to," said Thomas. "I mean, good bread of course . . ."

"With a toppings station," Emily added, "with only the nicest jams and marmalades, and the best cheese."

"Oooh, nice!" said Meg. "Can I sign up now to be a prisoner in your castle?"

"What was supposed to happen when the dragon bent over to pick up the flower?" asked Emily.

"The plan was that the elves would whack him over the head with the vase! That would knock him out long enough for Catherine to get out of the room and for them all to run down the stairs."

"That sounds like a good plan," said Emily.

"It's actually a terrible plan," said Meg. "Do you have any idea how hard it is to knock out a dragon? They have incredibly hard skulls."

"I knew that," said Thomas. "I knew it was an incredibly ineffective plan. I just didn't want to say anything."

"So Acorn had the vase and—"

"Wait a minute: you said they were still in the envelopes!" said Thomas.

"Another reason this was not a very good plan," said Meg. "Elves don't always think things through. I think at the last minute they managed to punch their arms out a little. They had been walking around in their envelopes for quite a while now, so the paper was getting, you know, not so strong and crispy anymore. So fortunately the vase rolled under the table, and Acorn got hold of it. When the dragon bent down to pick up the flower with his clumsy long claws, Acorn rushed out and swung the vase as hard as he could and bonked the dragon right on the noggin! He hit him so hard that the vase went flying out of his hands toward the stairs—right where you're sitting. The blow was nothing to the dragon, though. It was as if a mosquito had landed on his head! Still, it startled him a little, and as he turned to pick up the vase, Acorn realized that the dragon was going to see him! He panicked and ran straight into Catherine's open room!"

Meg got up and pushed the heavy wooden door open. "I don't think it's ever locked. I come up here sometimes, like when I have to decide about who's going to write this or that page and they're all nattering on, and I need a quiet place to think. I like it up here."

The three of them entered the room. It was filled with light and enveloped in stillness, and empty save for a few old wooden boxes stacked against the curving stone wall. There was a fireplace with an iron pot hanging in it, and two arched windows, one looking down into the courtyard and the other looking over the forest.

"What was in here when Mommy was here?" asked Emily.

"Oh, just some regular furniture—you know, a bed, a chair, a table, that sort of thing. Nothing elaborate." The children followed Meg to the window, which was big enough for the three of them to all look out of, leaning on their elbows.

"I wish there was still a bed. It would be fun to sleep up here," said Emily. "I would love to watch for elves, too! It's nice that there aren't any bars on the windows anymore. When did they take them out?"

"After your mother moved in, I would imagine," said Meg. "Though that, of course, would be getting ahead of ourselves."

"Getting ahead of ourselves, when there is so much going on in the present!" said Emily. "By which I also mean, the past. Meaning—"

"Meaning you want a little more story. Yes, I get it. You don't have to hit me over the head with a frying pan," said Meg.

"Or a pewter vase," said Thomas.

"Aren't you so very clever!" said Meg. "Fine, I'll keep going. So now Acorn was in the room with your mother, so terrified that the dragon would see him that he just zipped right under the bed! The dragon picked up the vase and the flower, got the tray back in order, pushed it into the room here, then shut the door and locked it like he always did. And that was the end of that little adventure.

"A despondent little envelope crawled out from under the bed. Acorn was just so terribly upset with himself. He felt he had been cowardly, running and hiding! He told Catherine how Robin had fallen into the moat and that Bonnie was stuck on the other side of the locked door and since he was now locked in with Catherine, he hadn't done one thing to help. All that work and nothing had come of it! 'And not only that,' he said, 'but I'm stuck in a ridiculous envelope!' Catherine helped him out and he apologized over and over for the sorry state of it all."

"Personally I think he's being very hard on himself," said Emily. "I mean, what else could he have done in that situation?"

"I completely agree," said Meg.

"Well, I don't!" said Thomas. "Maybe he could've picked up the vase and whacked the dragon in the ankles, which everyone knows is one of their weaker spots. And I just can't agree with hiding under the bed!"

"Perhaps he could've whacked the dragon in the ankles, but I don't think it would've helped much," said Meg. "And as I've said, perhaps dealing with a real-live fire-breathing dragon is a little scarier than you seem to think! Your mother also thought he was being very hard on himself, and told him so. While he was carrying on, she looked at the letter that was in the envelope with him, and then looked again, with a very thoughtful expression."

"We know that expression," Emily said to Thomas, who nodded. "I'll bet Mommy also rubbed her chin."

"And said 'hmmm,'" said Thomas.

"I also know that look and the 'hmmm'!" said Meg. "And then your mother said, 'Perhaps this letter will be some help to us. Maybe something good has come from this mission after all!'"

"What was in the letter?" asked Emily.

"Your mother wasn't sure," said Meg, "because it was written in a language she didn't know. But it intrigued her, and she was going to figure it out."

They were all quiet for a few minutes as they looked out over the meadow and the forest.

"It's nice up here," said Emily.

"It is, isn't it?" Meg agreed.

"But it makes me miss Mommy and Daddy a little bit."

"They'll be home soon enough," said Meg.

"And to think that the first we'll see them will be at the party!" said Emily. "I absolutely cannot wait! Don't you want to go to the party, even a little bit, Meg?"

"Not even a little bit. I'm very weary of this whole party business—trust me."

"Oh, Meg! I'm sure Mommy would love to see you, don't you think, after all these years?"

"I'm sure she would not."

Thomas shot Emily a look that begged her to stop, but she ignored it.

"But you can't still be mad at her about the tennis tournament, can you? She must've had a good reason not to come, don't you think? It must have been an emergency! Because Mommy's the kind of person who always does what she's supposed to—"

"It absolutely was not an emergency!" Meg snapped. "It was just an interview at the damsel college. That didn't sound like an emergency to me!"

"Oh. Maybe . . . I don't know. Maybe it was the only time—"

"It wasn't worth missing a tennis tournament for! It was the most important match of our lives. Yes, I got really mad about it, and we had a fight. I was so angry that she just abandoned me like that! I told her she was irresponsible, and other mean things, and she told me I was childish." Meg sighed. "The thing is, I *was* childish! I mean, really, I was a kid."

"That doesn't sound too bad!" said Emily. "Don't you think, you know, enough time has gone by? Maybe if you just went to the party and apologi—ow, hey!" she said as Thomas jabbed her in the ribs.

"There's more, if you really have to know, which I suspect you do. I won't get any peace until I tell you! Okay, look, so we had that one fight, and honestly I really did start to feel bad about the things I had said to her that weren't very nice. Like that she thought she was so smart and better than everyone else. It was mean and not even a little bit true. I wanted us to be friends again and I wanted to do something to show her that. So I got this great idea. I mean, I thought it was a great idea. Maybe it was just foolish."

"What did you do?" asked Thomas.

"Well, I told you I won that tournament, right? There was a big trophy, and every year they would put the names of the winners on it, and it would be displayed at the town hall. Krackengully had my name put on it, all fancy. But I started thinking: your mom and I had been partners forever, playing and practicing since we were little. So I decided to put her name on the trophy with mine."

"That's a really nice thing to do," agreed Thomas.

"I thought so!" said Meg. "So did Krackengully. He got me the trophy, and I scratched your mother's name on it with a nail. I thought it looked really good! Of course I've always had excellent penmanship."

"I see now that good penmanship can come in handy," said Emily.

"Absolutely!" said Meg. "I spent a whole afternoon doing it, in our backyard, and I left it there when I went in for supper. I was all set to take it to Catherine's house that evening. But when I came out of the house, I saw something I will never, ever forget." She paused here and looked out over the forest with a dreamy expression on her face as she remembered.

"When I came out," she said, "I saw the dragon right there in my own yard, lifting off from the ground and into the sky, flapping his huge wings—with the trophy in his claws! I yelled and threw a rock, but it was too late. He just flew away toward the woods and to his castle. I couldn't believe it."

"You saw the dragon yourself?" said Emily.

"I did! He had taken stuff before, from other people in the neighborhood, but I had never seen him up close like that. He was enormous. It was evening and the sky was turning red, and he was gleaming in the light. It was scary, but kind of beautiful, too, believe it or not. I'll never forget it.

"I ran all the way to Catherine's house. I was so excited

about seeing the dragon that I wanted to tell her, my best friend, all about it, and I wanted her to know that I'd put her name on the trophy, too. So I banged on her door and she came out and I told her everything. And guess what?"

"She thought you were making it up," said Emily, looking sideways at Thomas.

"Yes, she did. How did you guess? She said that I had made it all up, that there were no such things as dragons, and that she was going to college now and she was sick and tired of all my stories. She called me a liar and slammed the door in my face. And that was that."

"Oh," said Emily in a rather small voice.

They were all quiet for a minute as they looked out over the forest. Then Thomas said, "I like how when you're so high up, you can look down and see the tops of the birds' wings. You don't always get to see that."

"I like it, too," said Meg, and she smiled.

Chapter Eight

homas, I thought about it all last night. We really have to do something about the problem of Meg and Mommy not being friends!"

"I'm not sure you've noticed, but I'm actually eating breakfast right now. Can't this wait until after I'm done? And why is this even our problem?"

It was the next morning, a dark, rainy one, and the children were in their favorite place to eat when their parents weren't home, a cozy out-of-the-way corner of the kitchen with a window that looked out over the garden. It was a good place to watch the castle grown-ups get soaked as they trudged through the courtyard.

"Don't you think it's sad that they haven't been friends for all this time, just because of a teensy misunderstanding? I think it's tragic!"

"Emily, it's this porridge that's tragic—"

"Don't make fun. Anyway, I've got an idea about how we can get them to be friends again."

"I'm all ears," said Thomas between mouthfuls.

"So we get Meg to come to the party—"

"Already your idea is a failure! Meg said very clearly that she doesn't want to come, and I'm kind of getting the feeling that when Meg doesn't want to do something, Meg doesn't do something."

"Well, we just have to make her somehow! And we have to get her and Mommy to talk. You know, it will be a party and Mommy will be all happy, so it will be a good time for talking."

"But Meg won't be happy if we've tricked her into going! And you know what happens when witches go to parties and they're in bad moods: someone gets a spell cast on them and the whole thing's a disaster."

"I know you don't still think Meg is a witch," said Emily. "You're just trying to make fun of my plan, which you haven't even heard yet."

Thomas sighed heavily through his porridge. "All right, all right, go on."

"Remember Meg said, when she first started telling the story, that the dragon used to steal treasure and hide it in the castle? Maybe he hid Meg's trophy! I got the idea when Meg was telling us the story yesterday: maybe the dragon was using it as the vase he put the flowers in!"

"Don't you think Mother would've noticed the trophy with her and Meg's names on it? She said the dragon gave her flowers in it every day."

"But sometimes there are things right under our nose that we see every day but we don't notice, like Meg and those blue flowers."

"Still a stupid idea."

"Oh," said Emily quickly, looking down. "I guess you're right. As usual."

Thomas chewed for a moment, waved his spoon thoughtfully at his sister, and said, "But you know what? Maybe it's not such a stupid idea. Just because he wasn't using it as a vase doesn't mean it couldn't be in the castle somewhere!"

"You think so?" said Emily, bouncing back up in her chair.

"Sure, why not?"

"Oh, hooray! Then you'll help me find it? Because that's my idea: we find the trophy and we give it to Mommy, and she'll *have* to see that Meg was telling the truth. She'll understand that Meg was sorry, and they'll have a good laugh and say how they couldn't believe they were so silly for all these years, and then they'll be friends again and Meg will come to dinner all the time, and all the scribes, too! So let's think like a dragon. Where would he hide his treasure?"

Their search started in the castle's attic, which turned out be a mistake, because it was far too fascinating a place to look for one thing and one thing only, especially on a dark, rainy morning. The children quickly lost themselves in an odd and endless assortment of boxes, crates, trunks, and dusty old wardrobes.

"I had no idea there was so much stuff up here!" said Emily.

"We can't get sidetracked," said Thomas. "Remember, we're on a mission! We'll be up here for weeks if we go through everything."

After they had been up in the attic for at least three hours, and after they had found their favorite childhood game of picketypucks (which Emily won five games out of seven) and Thomas had found a serviceable old shield on which to practice painting his future coat of arms, and after Emily did not find her mother's wedding headpiece even though she was sure it must've been there somewhere, she flung herself into an old lumpy overstuffed velvet chair and announced, "I believe we may be looking in the wrong place."

"You think?" said Thomas. He was poking through a box of old jousting proclamations and wondering if he should hang one in his room for inspiration.

"Yes! I was thinking about how it would be so fun to take down one of the trunks of old hats and things, just for fancy dress-up, and then I said to myself, *Oh, what a bother it would be*, you know, dragging it down that skinny, rickety staircase we climbed up to get here, and then I thought that the dragon could never get up those stairs, right? Remember Meg said it was so hard for him even to climb the tower stairs, and those are nice and wide! He'd never come up here!"

"Hmm," said Thomas. "You may be on to something."

"Though maybe he could've given the trophy to Jerry to hide."

"Dragons always hide their own treasure," said Thomas with his usual air of authority concerning such matters. "I would check closets next."

"Especially ones with really high shelves that only a dragon could reach!" said Emily.

"We'll start with all the storerooms in the keep first," said Thomas, "and move to the outer towers after lunch."

"And if anyone asks us what we're looking for, we'll say my math homework," suggested Emily. "Because I really did lose it."

"Not again!" Thomas said with a sigh.

After conducting a thorough search of the kitchen pantry (where they found lots of nice fresh muffins, which Emily stuffed into her apron pocket—it had been a long time since breakfast, after all), they decided to look in the storeroom that held all the dishes for the banquets held in the Great Hall, because it seemed logical that the trophy could have sat there undetected for years. Who would notice it among all the gleaming serving bowls and candlesticks? But as they stood at the heavy door that led from the kitchen, Emily whispered, "I think there are people in there. Don't you hear voices? Maybe we should come back later."

"They're probably just setting up for lunch. No one will notice us. And if they do, you were doing your homework here yesterday, remember?" Thomas pushed the door open.

"And another thing I saw at a very fashionable party," a large man was saying loudly, "was that every table had a number, and people found their name on a card with their table number, so there was none of the usual milling around, which is so disorderly. And it was all very nicely done, of course."

The children were surprised to see Meg sitting at one of the long tables covered with papers, trying hard not to look completely bored and miserable. At the sound of their soft footsteps, she turned and immediately jumped up.

"Oh, my goodness, it's the noble children! Don't tell me there's been an accident. Did an inkpot explode? It was Reggie, wasn't it? Please don't tell me his ponytail caught fire again!"

"Uh," said Emily uncertainly. "We were looking—"

"For me, weren't you! Lady Dara sent you, didn't she, dear children? What's that? I need to come as quickly as I can?" Meg gathered up an armload of papers and hurried to the door. "I'm so sorry, Lord Gabriel. It seems there is an emergency! We'll have to continue this another time. I'll have the scribes start on the menus immediately—"

"But, Meg!" barked Lord Gabriel. "You can't leave—I have a lot more ideas to tell you!"

"Emergency, you know—can't be helped! Come along, my dears!" said Meg as she swept out the door, the confused children in tow.

"And don't let the fanciness slip just because we're running out of time!" Lord Gabriel shouted after them.

"Never!" Meg called back, leading the children out through the kitchen and into the courtyard.

Once outside, she laughed. "You kids just saved my life. I thought I was never getting out of there! Lord Gabriel's been telling me everything we still have to do for the past two hours: menus and name cards and table numbers and decorations . . . I was about to lose consciousness! Thanks for coming in at exactly the right moment!"

"You're welcome!" said Emily, running to keep up with Meg's quick pace. "Can we come back with you to the tower?"

"Sure, why not?" said Meg. "But couldn't you find something better to do on a rainy day like this?"

"We already played several games of pickctypucks," said Emily.

"And archery and all other outdoor activities are canceled again," said Thomas.

"Well, come along, then!" said Meg. "You can help me carry all these papers—all of Lord Gabriel's incredibly complicated party ideas. I just can't wait to show everyone, believe me."

Back in the tower room, Meg greeted the scribes. "Look who happened upon the most tedious meeting of my life, where I nearly succumbed to death by absolute boredom: our favorite apprentices!"

"Hooray!" they cheered.

"I think they might help us today, if we ask them nicely," said Meg.

"And I brought muffins!" said Emily, emptying her apron. The scribes cheered again.

"Today we will be drawing out menu cards for the tables, so the guests will know what sort of tasty delights are in store for them during the feast," said Meg. "And, as per Lord Gabriel, they are to be beautifully done, with all sorts of scrolly flourishes and whatnot, and no one is to draw faces on the tomatoes!"

"We got in trouble for that once," whispered Kitty to Emily.

"Reggie, can you run down to the storeroom and get some of that nice pokeberry ink? There were going to be peas on the menu, but Lord Gabriel says they changed it to beets, for reasons that remain vaguely unclear, so we need purple."

"Emily stuck peas up her nose once when she was little, so we don't ever have them!" said Thomas.

"I did not!"

"You did so!"

"I absolutely did not! Anyway, it was only one."

"Can we get the ink?" Thomas asked Meg. "I've always wanted to go down into the storeroom." He turned secretively to Emily and mouthed, "Trophy."

"Nah, we'll make Reggie go," said Meg. "It's too dark and creepy down there."

"And Reggie's not afraid of the cellar trolls," said Kitty. "He says you just sweep them out of the way with a broom."

"Cellar trolls? Now I really want to go down there!" said Thomas.

"What would your mother say if you got eaten by a cellar troll?" said Meg. "I don't need that kind of trouble. No, you kids can start drawing turnips."

"Turnips? Yuck!" said Emily.

"Emily's kind of picky," said Thomas.

"You don't say," Meg murmured. "I never would've guessed."

As she began to draw, Emily said, "Meg, you never explained yesterday what happened to Robin when he didn't make it through the portcullis and fell into the moat! I woke up in the middle of the night so worried, I couldn't get back to sleep!"

"Oh, I'm sorry about that! You needn't have worried. Elves are excellent swimmers, you know."

"But he was still in the envelope, right?"

"Well, yes, but you know once an envelope gets wet, it's quite easy to push your arms through it, so he could swim pretty well."

"But what about the crocodiles?"

"Like I told you before, elves aren't really afraid of crocodiles."

"I'm not, either," said Reggie. "They're really nothing to be afraid of, once you know what to do."

"Oh, Reggie, not punching them in the nose!" said Kitty.

"It works! And once I hit one in the nose with a frying pan. It was an especially large crocodile—"

"You were swimming with a frying pan?" said Meg. "That's weird even for you."

"I was swimming in the moat one day and I just found a frying pan in the muck at the bottom. I've found all sorts of weird stuff there over the years. It probably falls off the carts when they go over the drawbridge. Found a silver coin once!"

"Oh, really? When?" asked Kitty. "Because I just *lost* a silver coin."

Emily interrupted her turnip drawing to hastily scrawl a note and shove it over to Thomas. "The treasure might be *in* the moat!"

Meg began the story again. "Robin was in the moat, flailing about quite a bit. And the knights were all there on the grass when they saw this big envelope splashing around, so one of them, Sir Floyd, fished it out with a long stick. He thought it was a duck or a big white fish or something."

"Perhaps an albino baby crocodile?" suggested Reggie.

"I am quite sure he did not think it was an albino baby crocodile," said Meg. "Anyway, when he pulled Robin out of the water, Sir Floyd said something like, 'There ye be, wee woodland friend. Sit thyself down for a moment and take thyself a breath. How came ye to be a-floatin' around in the moat all wrapped as ye be in thy paper bonds?'"

"Knights don't talk like that all the time," said Thomas. "It's only for when they issue commands to dragons."

"But, Thomas, this was the olden days," Emily explained.

"Thank you," said Meg. "I like to imagine knights talking in a courtly way. Anyway, Robin couldn't quite answer because he was coughing up moat water. Even though he could swim, it *was* hard to do it in an envelope, and he may have swallowed a polliwog or two. Finally he spluttered out, 'I was on . . . a mission to try to rescue the fair damsel . . . but I fell . . . into the moat.'

"And Sir Floyd said, 'Nah, nah, wee elfy! Ye be far too small to aid in the rescue. Leave such important matters to we mighty knights, willst ye?' and the knights all laughed among themselves that someone so small thought they could dare make an assault on the castle. Another knight, Sir Boris, helped Robin out of his envelope and noticed that there was also a letter inside. 'Hmmm, wot's all this, then?' he said, and he read it. A moment later, he wadded up the wet paper into a ball and threw it angrily onto the ground.

"'It all be a monstrous lie!' he shouted to the other knights. 'The dragon, 'e's got no treasure! This be a most foul and nefarious bill from the bank saying the dragon is far, far behind on all of 'is taxes! There must be no treasure to speak of! Wot be the point o' riskin' our lives for this, then?'

"Cries of anger and dismay went up from the knights. Slowly they began to gather up their gear and load up their steeds, and one by one they trotted onto the path through the woods back to the village. 'Wait! Wait!' cried little Robin, running around from one to the other, soaking wet and quite upset. 'Where are you going? I'm sure the dragon still has treasure! You still have to help the damsel! She needs you! Please don't go!' But one by one the knights rode off. Finally Robin collapsed onto the ground, his head in his arms and his shoulders shaking with hopeless sobs.

"Then he heard a voice say 'Chin up, little chap.' Robin looked up. There was a knight standing there, his hand extended. 'Don't worry! I'll help you, and the fair damsel, too.'"

Meg paused dramatically. "And that knight was Sir Stephen."

"*Daddy!*" shrieked Emily. "I knew he would be in this soon! Oh, Thomas, this *is* going to be a romantic story after all!"

"Yes," said Meg. "It was inevitable. And now we have your mother up in her tower with Acorn, and Sir Stephen down below at the moat with Robin and the other elves. Since all the other knights were gone, they knew they had to come up with something really, really clever. First they needed a way to communicate with Catherine— they couldn't really have Sir Stephen stand at the foot of the tower and shout up to her, could they? And even if Stephen could get across the moat and over the wall without the dragon knowing, he would just be too conspicuous. And sure, the elves could climb up and down the tower to relay messages, but that was time-consuming and exhausting. So your father had this great idea. He visited his good friend the blacksmith in town and had him make two things: a pulley and a special arrow with a ring on the end, sort of like a big sewing needle, if you can imagine such a thing."

"I get it, but I'm not sure Thomas does."

"I know what a sewing needle looks like!"

"Unlike me, Thomas refuses to learn anything about sewing."

"Why would I have to? I'm going to be a knight."

"What about sewing on buttons and fixing rips in your horse's surcoat?" said Meg. "I'm sure there's a lot of upkeep. You should learn to do all these things yourself—more economical. How you haven't learned this from your mother, I have no idea."

"I'm good at sewing," said Emily. "Just a few weeks ago Mommy showed me how to sew a little kitty."

"Nobody cares, Emily!" said Thomas. "I want to get back to the story. It's just starting to get good."

"Okay, okay," said Emily. "Please go on, Meg."

"Sir Stephen took his new special arrow and looped a long rope through the ring at the end, tied it, then shot the arrow straight into Catherine's windowsill! And that was from the woods, so it was quite a shot."

"Wow! Father must've been a great archer in those days. Good thing he didn't shoot it through the window!" said Thomas.

"Like someone else we know!" said Myrta with a giggle.

"Moving on," said Meg quickly. "So you have the arrow stuck in the windowsill, and it's got a rope through it, and then back in the woods Sir Stephen took the pulley and nailed it to a tree and passed the other looped end over it. It was like they had sort of a very long clothesline, so they could pull messages back and forth! Clever, don't you think?"

"Wouldn't the dragon see it?" asked Emily.

"It was a thin rope, and the prevailing theory is that dragons don't see very well. Also I think that he was probably lying low, not rising majestically from the keep unless he absolutely had to. He probably wanted to stay away from the knights on his doorstep. He didn't like their pesky arrows much! He hadn't noticed yet that they had mostly all left."

Meg stopped painting for a moment and looked over at what Emily was doing. "Why are you drawing an eggplant? There are no eggplants on the menu."

"This is a fig."

"I see," said Meg. "Well, carry on, then." She continued: "The first thing Sir Stephen sent was some plain paper, because your mother didn't have any, and her first message back was that she wanted to translate the dragon's letter. In those days a damsel had to have a rudimentary knowledge of all the languages of the various forest folk, including dragons! Not like, you know . . ."

"The clearly inferior educations of the young folk of today, yes, yes, we get it," Emily said, waving her pen distractedly.

"Right! She knew how to read a little Dragon, and this writing was related. She guessed it was a foreign tongue. Basilisk, perhaps. There was one word that stood out to her, a word that is similar in all the languages of the larger reptiles. And that word was 'love.'"

"Ick," said Thomas automatically.

"Ignoring that," said Meg. "Catherine knew there was a book on Basilisk in the reference room at the library in town, so she asked Sir Stephen if he could look up the words she would copy out from the letter."

"Couldn't they just take the book out of the library and send it up to Mommy?"

"Well, it was a reference book, my dear. And don't think the elves didn't suggest they secretly 'borrow' it, but your mother wouldn't have that! You know how she is."

"Do we ever!" said Thomas.

Meg continued: "Your mother would write out a few words, send them down on the rope, and one of the elves would run through the woods to the library, where Sir Stephen set up shop at one of the big tables in the reference room. He would look the words up, write them down, and another elf would take the paper and run through the woods back to the rope and send it up again, and Catherine would work some more. Your mother had befriended a few birds by leaving crumbs on her windowsill for them, so sometimes a helpful bird would fly the message back and forth when the elves got tired of running around in the woods. It went on like this for a couple days, but the elves began to suspect that the letters *weren't* just translations, if you know what I mean!"

"I do, I do!" said Emily, fairly bouncing up and down in her seat. "They were *love notes*!"

"So gross," muttered Thomas, again automatically.

Chapter Nine

 little after dinner, the children put on their bathing suits and slipped through the castle's open front gate onto the drawbridge. The sky was just starting to turn from the palest delicate pink to dusky lavender, and the air was warm and heavy from the rain earlier in the day. The faintest breeze moved through the dark trees at the edge of the woods, and it was quiet except for birds softly calling from the field. A frog plopped lazily into the water from the weeds on the bank of the moat. Emily declared it the perfect night for swimming.

"Except that it isn't night," Thomas complained. "It's barely even evening."

"We wouldn't be able to see anything if it were any later," said Emily. "It will be kind of dark down there in the water as it is. I hope no one sees us and tells Grandmother!"

"Treasure hunting should be at least slightly dangerous," said Thomas, testing the water with a toe.

"The moat looks much greener than during the day. You don't think there's a lot of fish in there, do you?" said Emily, looking at the water nervously.

"Fish, no; crocodiles, maybe."

"Thomas! There are not! I wasn't even going to mention them!"

"Well, I hope there's lots of them, and snapping turtles, too! Here goes nothing!" he said, and jumped in. The dark water closed over his head. Emily waited for him to surface, but he did not.

"Thomas?" Emily called timidly.

She called again, a little louder this time. She could see nothing.

Then from beneath the drawbridge came a muffled splashing and thumping. "*Help!*"

"Thomas? Are you okay?"

"*Emily, helllllppppp!*"

Emily dove into the dark water and thrashed her way to the bridge, searching frantically for her brother, who had popped out the minute he heard her splash into the moat.

Thomas climbed back up onto the drawbridge, lay down flat, and poked his head underneath. "Looking for someone?" he said.

"Thomas! You're horrible!" Emily said, splashing him mightily. He laughed and jumped back in.

"Don't be mad! It was just to get you in the water!"

"I don't know why I believe you all the time." She splashed her brother again, then said, "Hey, it's not so bad, is it? It's really warm and nice once you get used to it!"

"I know! Let's start looking!"

Together they held their breath and dove to the bottom of the moat and searched through the murky weeds underneath the drawbridge. Eventually, though, even Thomas had to admit it was very hard to see much of anything. They felt through the weeds with their hands, but that ended when Emily was quite sure she touched something both slimy and alive and Thomas stepped on something that slithered away. They pulled themselves up out of the water and onto the bank, disappointed that they had no treasure (unless you wanted to call an old wooden button treasure—Emily did, but Thomas did not) but thrilled with their adventurous selves all the same.

"Name cards, kids, using your very, very best writing, because if there's anything a party guest likes, it's seeing their name all neat and pretty!" called Meg from her painting when the children came by after their lessons the next afternoon. "Myrta has all the little cards, and Dara will give you your list of names."

"Speaking of names," said Emily, "I was just thinking, you've never told us your last name, Meg! Because I was wondering if you were related to my friend Bessie. I heard her say once she had an aunt who—"

"Nice try!" said Meg. "I'm not telling, so you can't make me a name card because I'm *not going*. That's the night I have to sharpen all the pencils."

Dara laughed. "Don't you listen to her, Miss Emily!" she said. "You think Lord Gabriel would let his favorite scribe stay home? What if we lose a table number and people start milling about and no one knows where to sit? It will be an art emergency!"

"Oh, sure, I'm the only one who can draw a three," Meg grumbled, turning back to her painting. "Still not going. Not even Lord Gabriel can make me."

Emily sighed and began her first card. "And should we add a little scrolly flower, for extra fanciness?" she asked.

"You know it!" said Meg.

"And you'll keep telling us the story?" said Thomas.

"I don't know—I'm awfully busy with this painting, at a very hard part, doing all the frothy, lacy wedding dress bits."

"They did bring all those little tarts," pointed out Dara. "And I saw you eat three." She took one, winked at the children, and was out the door.

"So I did," said Meg. "I suppose I owe you that much, then!

"Catherine had translated the letter, and there had to be a way to use this information to their advantage, but how? All they had was one knight, one horse, a lady who was locked in a room, some secret information, and a handful of small elves—versus one large and scary fire-breathing dragon. Obviously they needed a truly effective and extraordinary plan. But the harder they tried, the more they came up with ideas that led nowhere, and elves grow bored with sitting and thinking. It was a beautiful summer night and the full moon was up—"

"You said it was a full moon at the beginning," Thomas pointed out. "It can't still be the full moon—it's at least a week later!"

"All right, it was past the full moon. What do you call it, when it's the squashier shape?"

"A gibbous moon. More specifically a waning gibbous moon, when it's getting smaller," said Emily.

"So they wanted to play their instruments and dance in the light of the waning gibbous moon, which, though accurate, sounds absurd," said Meg, rolling her eyes, "but Catherine said she was going to bed—"

"Mommy is soooooooo boring," said Emily.

"Perhaps, but she knew she was onto something with the letter. She wanted to read through it a few more times and really think about it—sleep on it even. The elves, though, were through with thinking for the night. They played a little bit of music, then slipped back through the tunnel in the wall, swam the moat, crossed the meadow, said good night to Sir Stephen, who was camped by the path, and skipped into the woods to play some tennis."

Meg paused here for a moment, looked around the room, then back at the children.

"The part I'm going to tell you next," she said, her voice dropping to almost a whisper, "I have never told another soul, not even this lot here."

The scribes looked up. "Oh, this should be good," said Myrta.

"What outlandish story have you *not* told us?" said Reggie. "Was it that time you saw the cat with the glowing eyes in the woods at night?"

"Or that time the owl asked you the riddle?" said Kitty.

"Nope, nope, none of those things," said Meg. "This next part actually has me in it! It happened when everything else was going on, but I didn't see how it fit into the whole story until much later. That long-ago summer, I was still playing tennis. I was, in fact, working for Mr. Krackengully, giving lessons to the littlest kids, helping to take care of the courts, that sort of thing. The night I'm telling you about, the night the elves went into the woods to play tennis, I was staying late to clean up. Before Mr. Krackengully left to go into town, he asked if I could mend one of the nets. I didn't want to stay there and do it because it was getting dark; I wanted to take it home and have my sisters help. So I untied the net from its posts and stuffed it into my apron pocket. It was then that I heard things."

"*Pixies?*" gasped Emily.

"I didn't know for sure," said Meg. "I just started getting this eerie feeling that I wasn't alone. I thought I heard laughter and voices from the path that were definitely not regular people. I didn't know if they were good or bad, if they were elves or fairies—"

"Or pixies!" said Emily.

"Right, or bogles or brownies or anything else! And you just never know—even the good forest folk can be mischievous. I wasn't going to run deeper into the woods with night coming on, so I decided to hide. You saw that big oak tree right next to the court? I scrambled up it, as high as I could go. And the little voices came nearer and nearer. I barely breathed and tried to blend into the tree.

"Soon they were there, right underneath me on the tennis courts! They merrily set about taking out all the rackets and balls I had just put away, and I could hear them talking and singing, and then bouncing a ball and hitting it back and forth to one another. Eventually I calmed down enough to where I could look down through the leaves and see them there on the ground under the tree. I sensed they were good forest folk, most likely elves—"

"Well, elves aren't so bad!" said Reggie. "As long as they weren't hobgoblins or those weird half-horse people, there really wasn't anything to be afraid of."

"Still, even the good-hearted forest folk don't like to be spied upon," said Meg. "I thought it was best to keep quiet. The first thing I noticed was that they are terrible tennis players! It's not their fault, really—you know, the rackets are just too big for them. Anyway, they kept hitting the ball straight up into the tree. Usually it would just rustle in the leaves and drop back again, but this one time it got wedged in the crook of a branch, just a few feet from me! I could hear them asking one another where it went. What if they looked up and saw me? I had to do something, so I inched myself up on the branch to dislodge the ball, and somehow the net in my pocket got snagged on a twig. I didn't notice until it was too late—the net just slipped right out of my pocket! I couldn't grab it or I would've fallen out of the tree myself! My heart stopped as it floated down and fell right on top of the elves!"

"I thought, well, that's it. They'll shoot me out of the

tree with arrows and take me away for a hundred years like I've heard elves do, and I'll never see my family again. I kept listening for their angry voices."

"Oh, Meg! You must have been so terribly frightened!" said Emily.

"Well, I was, but then I heard laughter! And I wasn't

scared so much. It was more, well, unsettling. Such a beautiful sound, though, like little bells. They seemed to think that the net falling on them was the funniest thing, and it wasn't even occurring to them to wonder where it had come from! I heard them talking excitedly among themselves, though I couldn't make out what they were saying. Then the voices trailed away and they were gone.

"I sat up in the tree for a good half hour, until it was dark. Then I climbed down and ran home as fast as I've ever run. But I've never told anyone till now."

"Wow!" said Kitty. "I can't believe you've never told us that one. But what about Krackengully? Didn't he wonder what you did with the net?"

"Oh, yeah, Krackengully," said Meg. "I just couldn't tell him. I didn't want him to think I was silly. I told him a giant eagle stole it from me on my way home because she wanted it for catching fish. I thought it made more sense at the time," she added with a shrug.

"Anyway—back to the regular story! After that incident, Catherine, Stephen, and the elves worked on a plan, and a few days later, they were ready. It started with your father, on top of his mighty steed, facing the dragon alone.

He stood in front of the drawbridge and demanded to be let in, according to the protocol. In a loud, brave voice, he called out, 'Dragon! Grant Me That I Mayest Access Thine Terrible Lair!'"

"Were the elves up in the beech tree, like last time?" asked Emily.

"No, they were somewhere else, but I can't tell you where. It was part of their secret plan, and I want you to be as surprised as the dragon was! I will tell you that they were listening, just as your mother was. They heard Jerry lower the drawbridge with that clicking sound—*click . . . click . . . click-click-click*, then *whomp!*—as the drawbridge thundered to the ground. They heard the horse's hooves clopping over the bridge, slowly and deliberately. It was the only sound on that hot, still afternoon. Then your father was there in the courtyard. 'Dragon! Prepare to Meet Thy Doom!' he called out in a voice even louder than before!"

Emily giggled. "I cannot imagine Daddy yelling that, not for serious!"

"All knights must be able to tell various things to prepare to meet their doom, and do so convincingly," Thomas explained with the air of someone who is vaguely annoyed that they have to keep explaining things. "It's a big part of being a knight."

"I know—I hear you practicing when you think no one's around. Poor Teddy has met his doom many times!"

"I do not still have a teddy, and even if I did—"

"He does so," said Emily to the others.

"That is so sweet!" said Myrta.

"It isn't sweet because I don't," said Thomas.

"He absolutely does."

"*I do not!*"

"Children!" said Meg wearily, rapping her brush against the top of her painting. "I can paint and talk at the same time, but I have a hard time painting and listening to squabbling at the same time."

"Ooh, that reminds me to look at how the painting is coming along!" said Emily, getting up and going around to see.

"All right, what's wrong now?" said Meg. "I can see by your furrowed brow that you are displeased."

"It all looks so beautiful—it really does!"

"But . . . ?"

"Well . . . it's just a tiny detail, hardly worth mentioning."

"But Emily must mention it!" said Thomas.

"Don't you think the embroidery on the collar of Mommy's dress is . . . I don't know, a weird color? It's a very peculiar purply gray."

"Your grandmother showed me the dress, and that's the color it is."

"But don't you think it could've faded a bit? Maybe it used to be . . . more blue."

Meg sighed in an extremely exaggerated manner, then said, "All right, all right, the happiness of you little nobles is, of course, my only concern. Let's try it a little more blue."

"Oh, that's perfect! Doesn't that really bring out the blue in Mommy's eyes?"

"I suppose," said Meg grudgingly. "But it will really be a lot of bother to change it all."

"You don't mind, though," said Emily, getting back into her seat.

Meg sighed again and dutifully continued to paint.

"So your father told the dragon to meet his doom, and

then the next thing everyone heard was the great whoosh-ing sound of the dragon's enormous wings, the slow heavy beating of the air as he rose majestically from the keep and landed in the courtyard across from your father. Even though they had a plan—and a good one, they believed—I imagine the elves and your parents couldn't have helped but feel a bit uneasy. The dragon must've been a terrifying sight to see, standing there with smoke coming out of his nose and his scales gleaming golden red in the sun—"

"Funny you never really told us what color the dragon was before," said Emily as she put another name card on the pile. "I always imagined him sort of greenish black, like the crocodiles."

"Oh, no, he was a beautiful fiery golden red. He looked quite handsome on the green grass. I mean, you know, for being terrible and scary and all that. There he was, right underneath your mother's tower—"

"You didn't tell us Daddy's horse's name, either," said Emily.

"It's Daisy!" said Thomas unexpectedly. "Don't you remember Father told us? His first horse when he was a knight was a mare named Daisy."

"Daisy, there you go," said Meg. "On the other side of the courtyard was your father, on his gallant steed, Daisy, in one hand his reins, and in the other his battle lance. And there they stood, facing each other."

"This is what I've been waiting for all along!" said Thomas. "We're at the best part now!"

"This seems like an excellent place to stop, then," said Meg.

"What?" said Thomas. "Why?"

"I ran out of blue paint, so I have to go grind up some rocks and make some more—you know how perfect it all must be! Don't want anyone's eyes to not look sparkly blue," said Meg. "I'm sure you have to go work on your dance routines and everything anyway. All must be perfect for the party, you know!"

"Can't you tell us a tiny bit more? At least give us a hint?" said Thomas.

"Nope, nope!" said Meg. "I want you to be just as surprised as the dragon!"

Chapter Ten

on't you get it, Emily?" said Thomas. "Meg not telling us what happens next because she 'wants us to be surprised' is just code for she has no idea, and needs another night to think of something! It couldn't be more obvious that she's just making the story up as she goes along and has been all this time! I don't know how you can't see that." It was the next day right after lunch, and the children had renewed their search in the moat on this hot and humid afternoon, more sensibly during daylight hours.

"Well, I think it's all real," said Emily, treading water beside him.

"Speaking of 'real,' I think it's really annoying that some of the things in her story are real and some are pretend, and you can't tell what's what. She just fills in pretend stuff around the real things, or real stuff around the pretend things. Lazy storytelling, if you ask me. Either it should be all real or all pretend, not this half-and-half business—"

"*Look out below!*" came a voice, followed by a flash of blue and orange stripes overhead, then an enormous *ker-SPLOOOOSH!* When the water settled, a familiar face burbled to the surface.

"Hi, kids!"

"Reggie!" squealed Emily in delight.

There were three more *ker-splooshes*, and soon the moat was filled with scribes, all in the most outrageously colored bathing suits.

"We heard you out swimming, and it was so hot in there today, we couldn't resist!" said Myrta.

"Is Meg coming, too?" said Emily.

"Oh, no, Meg's at a meeting with Lord Gabriel and Dara," said Kitty. "She'll never know."

"And if she knows, she won't mind," said Lester.

"Swimming was a great idea," said Kitty. "It was baking hot in there today—all our paper was getting soggy. We needed a break."

"We should swim over on the other side of the castle," said Reggie. "Fewer weeds."

"But it's so fun to dive off the drawbridge," said Thomas.

"And we really like looking for . . . things," said Emily. "You know, Reggie, like you said, stuff that's fallen off the carts into the moat."

"I love looking for stuff!" said Reggie. "Next to crocodile hunting, it's pretty much my favorite hobby. Come on,

I'll show you where I've found the most things—it's on the other side of the bridge, right by the gatehouse."

The children and the scribes swam under the bridge. They spent the next hour diving and searching through the mud and weeds and came up with a surprising number of modest treasures: a few pennies, a tin cup, and a spoon Reggie swore he lost the summer before when the scribes had a secret picnic. Eventually the scribes climbed out of the moat and lay on the bridge so they could dry off before going back to work, and when the children realized they weren't going to find the trophy, they joined them.

"We should go back inside, but the sun feels so good!" said Myrta.

"I know, the last thing I want to do is draw more broccoli!

So boring," said Lester. "We're never going to be done with these infernal menus."

"We'll go with you!" said Emily. "We want to hear more of the story when Meg comes back. She has to finish before tomorrow!"

"Yes, it's very exciting," said Kitty.

"I'll say it is!" said Thomas. "Now we're at a more real part, with my father set to fight the dragon—that part I can believe, unlike some of that other stuff, like the elves and the tennis courts and the dragon and the flower in the vase. Don't you think it's annoying how she'll say any nonsensical thing just to further the plot, whether it makes any sense or not?"

"Oh, I don't think Meg does that!" said Myrta. "Though sometimes you wish she would! Like when she goes on and on. Remember that time she told us about the wild boar that got into the trash? And I don't know why, but she had to tell us everything it ate, starting with apple cores and bread crumbs and chestnuts, all the way up to zucchini! Funny how I remember everything, though."

"Right, she said it ate halibut!" said Reggie. "Which is totally unbelievable—everyone knows wild boars are strict vegetarians."

"And why would a wild boar get halibut? We've never had it. And if we've never had it, why would it be in the trash?" added Lester. "That particular story was definitely suspect."

"Thomas, are there halibuts in the moat?" whispered Emily, looking around anxiously.

"There's something a little different about this story," said Reggie. "Like it's really going somewhere. We've heard a lot of Meg's stories. But I never heard the one yesterday, with the elves."

"Speaking of elves, this is my biggest question of all," said Thomas. "How does Meg even know this story? Besides the part she's in, I mean. She doesn't talk to our mother anymore, so is she claiming that the elves talk to her?"

"Meg really does know an awful lot of people," said Kitty.

"She does! And they're not always necessarily even people!" said Reggie. "Like, remember last year, she told us she was doing a book club with a selkie and a couple of werewolves?"

"This is my point exactly," said Thomas. "Meg seems to tell an awful lot of fibs. How do you ever know if she's telling the truth? Is any of the story she's telling about our mother true at all?"

The scribes were quiet for a second, then Kitty said, "Well, I think it's sort of true that Meg used to be good at tennis. Didn't we see her with her racket that time, when she had to get that giant snake out of the woodshed?"

"Yes, but remember Meg also said she was good at blusterball, and we all know from the castle summer picnic that this is definitely not true," Lester pointed out.

"Did you actually *see* her play tennis, or did she just *tell* you?" asked Thomas, but by now the scribes were too busy discussing what had and had not happened at the castle summer picnic five years ago, and his question went unanswered.

"Uh-oh," said Reggie, looking up.

"What's going on out here?"

Meg was standing in the gatehouse, looking down at all of them and obviously trying very hard to look angry. She had a huge bundle of papers in her arms.

"I can't believe you're all out here having fun when I've been in a horrible meeting for the last hour! Do you have any idea how much more we have to do before tomorrow?" she said, waving the papers at the scribes. "Plans for giant paper flowers and stars and let's not forget the numbers on the tables—"

"We weren't out here that long," said Reggie. "We were just going back in anyway."

Thomas and Emily started to get up with the others, but Meg laughed. "I didn't mean you! You guys are kids. You *should* be in the moat on a beautiful hot summer day! Stay in, stay in."

"See you tomorrow, kids!" said Myrta.

"When you get back, start mixing up all the different paint you can find," said Meg to the scribes. "Lord Gabriel wants us to make an enormous banner that says Happy Anniversary! with every letter in a different color. He thinks it will add winsome charm." When the scribes disappeared into the gatehouse, she sat down on the drawbridge and took her shoes off. "While they're getting everything ready, I'm going to sit here and put my feet in the water. It really does look so cool and nice."

"That gives you enough time to tell us what happened with Father and the dragon!" said Thomas. "Please?"

"I guess I could tell you a little more. We did leave it at sort of an exciting part, didn't we? Why don't you both come and sit up here. The next part of the story is sort of complicated, so I'm going to draw it out for you." Meg unrolled some of the paper and flipped it over to the blank side, then fished around in her pocket for a stubby bit of pencil. The children hoisted themselves out of the moat and onto the drawbridge.

"So where were we?" said Meg as she leaned over the paper and started to draw. "Your father and the dragon were facing off in the courtyard, right? Over here, under the tower, is the golden-red dragon, glistening brilliantly in the sun, not that you can tell from my pencil drawing, of course. Then over here is your father on his gallant steed, Daisy. Forgive me: I'm not very good at horses."

"I see that," said Thomas. "First of all, you forgot her surcoat. And don't forget Father's heraldic device. It's—"

"Look, young man, I'm doing my best with this very un-sharp pencil," said Meg. "You'll just have to imagine the tiny details, all right? And here's your mother, way up in her tower, ready to watch the unfolding spectacle. Let me give your father his lance."

"Wrong hand," said Thomas. "Father holds it in his right."

"*Meg!*" bellowed a voice from the gatehouse. "You forgot the list of entertainments!"

"Hold on, kids," said Meg wearily. "Lord Gabriel beckons. I'll be right back." She put down the pencil and quickly trotted out of sight into the gatehouse.

"I'm going to fix the dragon for her—it's awful," said Thomas. "Looks more like a giant wildebeest. She didn't even give it the right number of horns."

"Well, Meg actually saw the dragon, and you haven't!"

"I'm still going to fix it."

"Then I'm going to pick some flowers. I'll make Meg another wreath."

When Meg reappeared a few minutes later with even more papers, she seemed genuinely pleased with the improvements. "Well done, Thomas! You seem to have really caught the aspect of the dragon there! Look at those terrible eyes! And the plates along the back—very graceful!"

"I told you Thomas likes to draw. He doesn't like anyone to know. I have no idea why," said Emily, already busily weaving flower stems.

"It has to be the right things," said Thomas. "Not, you know, flowers and such."

"I think you should keep it up," said Meg. "Look at the dragon there, all tense and ready to spring! I like the smoke billowing from his nostrils!"

"Thank you," said Thomas.

"So here is the very fine improved dragon, so powerful and angry, ready to lash out with his sharp claws, and here are your father and Daisy, ready to advance," said Meg as she quickly and lightly sketched a new knight and horse, closer to the dragon. "Daisy started with a graceful canter, then slowed, as your father moved the lance to his proper hand, now in striking position. Then they trundled on, a little quicker this time, but not much."

"Why is Father so hesitant?" said Thomas, caught up in the drawing. "You can't give the dragon too much time to think—you have to strike fast! They're crafty but easily confused. You can't let them get comfortable!"

"Your father had one eye on the dragon, but the other eye—well, he was keeping that one on Catherine, up in the tower."

"Because he was so much in love?" asked Emily.

"Well, yes, partly that, but also partly because he had to wait for the next part of the plan. Your father had to keep the dragon on his toes. He raised his lance, and Daisy trotted in closer and faster, and just as they lunged, the dragon lashed out with his great terrible claws! Daisy nimbly corkscrewed this way and that." On another part of the paper, Meg drew another horse, knight, and dragon. "Then your father expertly dodged the claws and gave the dragon a backhanded swat on the nose with his lance, before wheeling about and dashing away."

"That's Father's signature move!" said Thomas. "He's actually teaching me it, with the quintain. It's called Side-tracking Backhanded Snout Whacking!"

"To think I somehow knew that," said Meg, "without even knowing what a quintain is!"

"It's for knight training," explained Thomas. "Sort of like a false assailant that swings at you."

"Your father and Daisy kept at it this way for some time," said Meg. "Charging, lunging in, but then pivoting back and retreating at the last second, always keeping out of reach of the dragon's claws!"

"Excellent tactics!" said Thomas admiringly. "Tiring out the dragon, never letting him rest, not letting up for a second!"

"While your father was keeping the dragon thus occupied at the foot of the tower, way up at Catherine's window, something was happening!" And here Meg began to draw more quickly. "From out of the window came twenty little elves, each with a tiny parachute made from a bedsheet, dyed blue! All slowly drifting down, holding on to the edge of a giant net made from four tennis nets sewn together, also dyed blue! The elves had picked arm-loads of those little blue flowers, and Catherine had made dye and had dyed everything so the dragon wouldn't see them out of the corner of his eye."

"I love this!" screeched Emily, clapping. "Did Mommy dye the elves' outfits blue, too? At the beginning of the story, you said they were in the colors of the forest—so the dragon would see that! They need to be in blue outfits, too!"

"Well, it's very hard to dye dark-green things light blue," said Meg. "Practically impossible! Your mother actually had to make the elves new little outfits. It was a good thing she knew how to sew and had all her sewing things with her when she got caught! First she cut up the blanket on her bed to make them all little pants and tunics. Then she told the dragon she was cold at night and needed more. I think she used every sheet and blanket in the whole castle! He wouldn't have thought a thing of it—not understanding how warm-blooded creatures are, you know."

"That is so brilliant!" said Emily.

"Did it work? Did they catch the dragon?" asked Thomas impatiently.

"Well, it certainly seemed like a good plan. But sometimes even good plans don't work perfectly! It's hard to catch a dragon with a net. They managed to half cover him, and they scrambled to stay on, but one wing broke free, and— wait a minute. There's too much drawing on this one now. I'm going to get another sheet and start the dragon again."

Meg tossed that piece of paper aside and started on a fresh one. "Okay, here's the dragon, with this giant net wrapped around him and elves clinging to him! And he was furious. One wing was free, and the other wing, under the net, was trying to beat, and the elves were barely hanging on as the dragon slowly and awkwardly began to rise into the sky! Your mother was terrified the elves would be hurt, so she cut the rope that went through the arrow in the windowsill and yanked it free of the pulley. She quickly made a lasso and threw it as the dragon flew past—and she managed to catch the dragon by the tail!" Meg was talking very fast now and drawing even faster. "Your mother had caught the dragon, but she knew she wouldn't be able to hold on to it herself, so she threw the rope down to your father. He was wearing his heavy armor—"

"Even so, Father wouldn't be able to hold on to a flying dragon!" said Thomas.

"The rope was making the dragon more angry—he was caught by the tail, which infuriated him, and he was half covered in nets and elves! He turned his head and tried to blow fire at the elves to get rid of them, but then he wasn't watching where he was going and he crashed into the flagpole on top of the tower!"

Meg was sketching very quickly now, and even this new paper was nearly covered. "He thrashed and thrashed and the elves clung even harder, but Catherine was terrified he would break free and throw them off. So she called to her bird friends, and they came and grabbed the loose ends of the net.

They flew around and helped to bind the dragon even tighter, making his wings useless! He was sort of hanging by the rope, which had caught on the flagpole, and it looked like he would crash to the ground, taking the elves with him. Your father couldn't hold him suspended himself! Then, just then, miraculously, the outside door to your mother's tower flew open and all the knights and horses who had been imprisoned by the dragon burst from the dungeon!"

"I *knew* he didn't eat them!" Emily said joyously.

"But how—?" began Thomas.

"It was Bonnie, wasn't it?" said Emily. "She was in the

castle the whole time! She found the dragon's keys and let them all out!"

"That is exactly what happened! The knights sprang out and grabbed the rope. Soon there were lots of knights and their horses hanging on, and the last horse was Neal, who as I said before, was very sturdy, and he had the end of the rope in his teeth. And all of them were enough to keep the dragon suspended upside down with his wings wrapped tight around his body, bound with nets and elves and parachutes. So there he hung, right in front of your mother's window. He may have been upside down, but he could still blow fire!"

Meg took a breath and put her pencil down. "Look at that paper," she said. "Completely used up! There's no room left to draw, so it looks like the end of the story will have to wait."

"Are you kidding? We have to know what happened!" said Thomas.

"The dragon is right in front of Mommy—she could get roasted! You can't stop now!" pleaded Emily.

"I absolutely can so stop," said Meg. "Ran out of room on the paper. Who knows what will happen to your mother now!"

"We'll get you some more!"

"No, no. This is a good place to stop. You'd better run along and practice your dance moves for the party. I don't want you to not practice and have it be all wrecked on my account."

"But, Meg! You have to finish!"

"I will! Just not right now. Look at all these things I have to do for that blasted party," said Meg, rifling through her papers. "Here's the latest: we have to make programs of the entertainment. I saw both your names on the list, you clever children!"

"If you come to the party, you can see me dance and you can hear Thomas play the lute!"

Meg smiled. "You know, I think I would like that. And we always do have a lot of fun . . . Wait until you hear Reggie sing! I was just starting to think that maybe I'll go to the party after all."

"Oh, Meg! We knew you'd come! You can come sit at the head table with us, and you can see all the performers right up close! You can sit next to Mommy—"

"Look, I'll come, but that's as far as it goes." Meg began to roll her papers up. "I'll just stay in back with the gang. I know you think if I come to the party, your mother and I will magically become friends again, but it's not going to happen, as much as you'd like it to. Sometimes you just don't stay friends with people your whole life."

"But how can you still be mad at her after all this time?"

"Emily," Thomas said softly, but his sister ignored him.

"I know you were upset because Mommy didn't believe you about the trophy, but that was so long ago! Plus Mommy saw the dragon, so maybe she did believe you, after that."

"The fact that your mother found out about the dragon didn't change anything," said Meg. "She's the one who's still mad! I've tried to talk to her over the years when I see her in the castle, but she just walks away. She doesn't want to be friends."

"I'm sure she does. Mommy would love to talk to you—I just know it!" Emily insisted.

"Your mother's holding the grudge, not me! She doesn't want to see me at the party. She didn't even invite me to her wedding! She invited the whole neighborhood, everyone in town, practically! But not me. And we were the best friends out of anyone."

"But—but, Meg," Emily stammered. "She *must* have invited you! You said yourself the mail carrier back then wasn't as good as the one today. Your invitation must've gotten lost in the mail!"

"Ha, a fine excuse! Your mother clearly didn't want me at her wedding, and she won't want to see me now. Look, it's her big night and I'm happy for her. I'll just stay out of her way. I'm good at that sort of thing."

Even though Thomas was squeezing her elbow, silently willing her to stop, Emily tried one more time. "Meg, please sit with us. Mommy will love to see you. If you both just talk, I'm sure you can make up! And look, I made you a flower wreath to wear at the party. You'll be so pretty! I'll make one for Mommy, too, and you can match—"

Meg abruptly got to her feet. "I actually have to get back

to work now. So why don't you kids run along, go practice your musical selections—"

"We'll come help," said Emily.

"We're fine. We don't need any help. Look, it's a beautiful day. What kind of kids want to draw broccoli in a horrible dark basement on a day like this? Good grief, you're just kids. You should go be kids." She turned back to look at them one last time before she disappeared into the gatehouse. "It's all okay. I just have to get back to work, all right? Go play, why don't you?"

"Well, now you've done it," said Thomas glumly. "You pushed and pushed and now she'll never talk to Mother."

Emily sighed and looked down into the water. "There's *got* to be a way!"

"We can't just make them be friends again," said Thomas.

"Good thing I have tapestry weaving now," said Emily. She stood up. "I've got some thinking to do."

Chapter Eleven

homas! I've been running around looking for you for an hour!" said Emily breathlessly as she popped back out through the gatehouse onto the drawbridge. It was later now, almost dinnertime. "Have you been here the entire afternoon?"

Her brother looked up and shrugged. "I guess so."

"I can't believe you're still lying here! What are you doing, drawing?"

"Yeah, Meg dropped some papers and her pencil when she stomped off. It's sort of nice being out here alone."

"Wait, are you drawing . . . flowers? You are! You're drawing the flowers from the wreath she forgot!"

"So what? I can draw flowers if I want. Good grief, I knew you'd be weird about it."

"It just seems so unlike you."

"Well, I'm not drawing them for *me*. Maybe I'm making Mother an anniversary card—"

"The anniversary, right! That's why I came to find you! Thomas, I was thinking about the party all afternoon while I was working on my tapestry, and I came up with a solution—"

"Oh, yeah? So did I! My solution is called Let's Keep Out of It."

"No, Thomas, listen! I came up with the perfect way to get Mommy and Meg to talk to each other again!"

"I really think we should just let this go. Did you ever think that maybe things could get even worse?"

"But this is a really good idea! Just listen, okay?" Emily sat down next to her brother, took off her shoes, and dangled her feet in the moat. "As we know, the problem is that Meg thinks Mommy didn't invite her to the wedding because she was still mad. But Mommy couldn't have been mad at Meg for lying about the dragon, because Mommy saw the dragon. The reason has to be that she didn't believe Meg about the trophy!"

"Yes, yes, we've been through this already," said Thomas impatiently. "We tried to find the trophy, but in case you haven't noticed, the party is tomorrow, and our prospects of finding it are pretty dim. It would take weeks to search the whole moat, if it's even in here at all."

"You're right: we're probably not going to find it in time. But, Thomas, what if, instead of the trophy, we bring the one person who knows about it and can explain everything?"

"But that person is Meg! And if Mother didn't believe Meg then, why would she now? You know"—his voice dropped to a whisper as he looked around furtively—"how stubborn Mother can be."

"Not Meg. Mr. Krackengully! Don't you remember? He gave the trophy to Meg so she could scratch Mommy's name on it. He can back up Meg's story. Mommy will remember him, and he's a grown-up, so she'll believe him. Remember when we went into the woods and saw the little house with smoke coming out of it? Meg said he still lived there!"

"We never saw him! It could've been trolls or wizards."

"Of course it's him!"

"But remember what Meg said: the scribes can't invite anyone who's not on the list! They take their job very seriously, and I'm pretty sure there was no Mr. Krackengully on the list!"

"Maybe *they* can't invite him, but *we* can!" said his sister slyly. "We'll make an invitation that looks just like the scribes', and there will be hundreds of people. No one will notice an extra guest! We'll just sneak into the woods in the dead of night and leave it at his house."

"I do like the dead of night part," said Thomas. "Do you

really think he'd come to the party? It's tomorrow!"

"He's probably like you and Daddy and doesn't need much time to put his outfit together," said Emily briskly, and so it was decided.

"Again, this isn't the dead of night," Thomas complained as they crossed the drawbridge after dinner.

"Well, you can think of it as the dead of evening. We have to be back before the drawbridge closes," said Emily.

"Dead of night would be much better."

Emily sighed, thinking again of the gryphons. "It's *almost* night. And doesn't it look like rain? It'll probably even get dark earlier than usual. And we're being sneaky about it, so that's something, right?"

The children had indeed been vague about where they were going after dinner, telling their grandmother, as she did some mending, and their grandfather, as he read the day's proclamations, only that they were going out to play with some of the other castle kids, and that seemed to go over quite well. Still, they took care that no one saw them pass through the gatehouse and over the bridge.

"Lucky for us the guards really do play an awful lot

of cribbage, and they invite old Oskar," Emily said, and Thomas did have to agree with that.

"Not that technically we're *not* allowed to go over the drawbridge after dinner, though," he was quick to add. "I mean, we can really go whenever we want."

"Of course," said Emily. "But it *is* more fun to make sure no one sees us!"

Together they ran through the long grass of the meadow, then dove behind the big beech tree. When they were certain no one had seen them, they made a break for the woods. Even though it was barely evening, it was a little darker under the trees than they'd thought it would be. "Isn't it so nice and cool here now?" said Emily. "And listen to the birds! Even more than last time."

"No dillydallying, Emily," said Thomas, "And no losing our heads and running around all crazy if we think we hear pixies or gryphons or squirrels or anything! We're on a serious mission. We get there and back and that's it. Especially since it might rain later."

"Okay," said Emily. "We'll walk fast."

"If it isn't dark yet," Thomas said as they stepped onto the path, "how are we going to make sure we can get the invitation to Krackengully without him seeing us? I'm sure he isn't in bed yet."

"Well, old people do like to go to bed early," Emily observed.

"Mother and Father don't! Look how late they stay up reading!"

"Maybe he'll be in bed reading, too. That would work out fine," said Emily. "We'll just sneak up all quiet and put it through his mail slot in the front door. He'll never see us."

The children continued on the path, Emily recounting all the landmarks: the soft beautiful ferns, the mushrooms, the gooseberry bushes. "Even though it's darker now, I'm happy all these things are still here," she said.

"Oh, Emily, you're not scared, are you?"

"No, not really. It's just, you know, nice to see all the same things from the other day, that's all! And since we're not worried about getting lost, this is a good time for us to discuss our plans for the party."

Thomas sighed. "I guess there's no escaping your plans."

Emily smiled. "Nope! Okay, you know how whenever there's a fancy party, the guests get in a really long line to greet whomever the party is for?"

"Oh, sure, that's when we generally get hugged and kissed by all our various aunties—yuck."

"Right! What we do is make sure Mr. Krackengully is in line well before Meg. He should be almost at the front of the line, so Mommy will see him right off. She'll be so happy! He'll tell her about Meg and the trophy and how she really did put her name on it—"

The children were at the hill that led up to the ridge now. As they climbed, Thomas said, "Hold on, Emily! Are we really going to talk to him first, and tell him what to tell Mother? And this was all a really long time ago. What if she doesn't even remember him?"

"Oh, you know she will! Mommy remembers everyone! And people always talk about old times at parties," said Emily with certainty. "And then when she's thinking about tennis and the happy times from when she was a kid, she'll start thinking about Meg in a more kindly way. I know how these things work, Thomas. And by the time Meg gets up to her in line, she'll be ready to hear her apology." They were traveling along the ridge now, and looking down through the trees and tangled bushes, they could see the leaf-covered clearing.

"And how are we even going to get Meg into the line? You remember what she said. Oh, look! Remember when we both fell down the hill? We must've tripped over this log here. Let's roll it out of the way. I bet if we keep going, we'll find a proper way down," said Thomas.

He was right. A little farther along, the path turned down the hill that led to the clearing. It had probably been open and well traveled in days gone by; now it was overgrown with grasses, bushes, and vines. Still, it was an easier way down than the tumbles they'd taken the other day.

As they picked their way to the courts, Emily said, "I'm trying to think what it must've been like for Mommy when she was young to come down through the trees and see it all here. It must've been so fun to play tennis in the woods with all her friends. I wish we could!"

Thomas smiled. "Yeah, me too." Then he said, "Now, look, Emily, there's the little house there. You go put the invitation through the mail slot, since you're littler and quieter. I'll keep watch from over here. If I see anything suspicious, I'll hoot like an owl, all right?"

"Got it," said Emily. She crept stealthily through the undergrowth on the perimeter of the court to the dark, mossy front steps of the house and pushed the envelope through the mail slot of the front door. Then she ran back to Thomas, and the two of them fled back up the hill and into the darkening woods.

The children were laughing and making plans for further adventures when they came out of the trees and into the meadow and up to the castle. Their laughter stopped when they came to the moat.

"The drawbridge is up! Emily, you said it would be down! That was the whole point of leaving so early!"

"Well, I *thought* it would be down. I . . . don't know exactly when it goes up, I guess."

"What are we going to do now?"

"I guess we'll have to yell and try to get Oskar to lower it, or maybe Frederico is in the mailroom and he'll hear, but then he'll know we were out and so will everyone else."

"There's got to be another way," said Thomas.

"Well, what would the elves do?" said Emily.

Thomas grinned. "That's it! We find the tunnel in the wall Meg's always talking about and swim! I've always wanted to swim in the moat at night—that didn't count the other day. Come on, I think it will be down along the wall this way, past the mailroom and the next tower. Meg said it comes out into the garden, remember?"

"What about the crocodiles? I know we didn't see any before, but . . ."

"Then we do what Reggie says: punch 'em in the nose! Come on, Emily. I'll swim with you. It will be easy! And it's starting to rain. We would've gotten wet anyway. What's a little more water?"

"Okay, I'll do it! I won't be scared if you stay with me."

They walked slowly along the moat, looking carefully for the tunnel in the castle wall.

"So, if we find it, will that mean that you believe Meg's story about the elves?"

"Not necessarily—I'll just believe that Meg and the scribes swim in the moat a lot when they're supposed to be working. Oh, look, I think that's it! There, through the weeds. I can't believe we've never seen it before!"

"Uh, it looks kind of dark," said Emily nervously, staring at the black half circle at the base of the wall, nearly covered by water grasses.

"Of course it does—it's a tunnel!" said Thomas. "Nothing to worry about, though. It's just a big pipe we have to crawl through. I mean, how long can it be?"

"Think about it," said Emily. "Think how thick the walls are, then add in the width of the corridor. It's probably fifteen feet long at least!"

"I hope you're not getting cold feet," Thomas said. "If you're too scared, I'll go through myself and then get someone to open the drawbridge."

"If you can do it, I can do it! It'll just take a few minutes, right? And there's plenty of room in there, right? I mean, we'll have our heads above water. It just goes straight through and that's it, right?"

"Of course—we'll be through in a minute!"

Thomas took off his shoes, tied the laces together, and threw them over the wall. Emily took hers off, too, and threw them, but they fell short and plopped into the moat. "Oops," she said.

"Good thing Mother's not home," said Thomas.

"I didn't like those shoes anyway," said Emily.

Together they stepped into the moat. The water was cool and actually felt quite wonderful in the warm summer night. They paddled next to each other through the weeds and lily pads. The moat was about twenty feet wide there, and they got across quickly.

"So far so good," said Thomas, treading water as they paused at the mouth of the tunnel. It was raining a little harder now. "Well, let's get out of the rain, then," he said, trying to sound cheerful as they pushed through the weeds and ducked under the stone arch into the pipe, which was about six feet across. "Watch your head!"

"Shouldn't we be able to see all the way through?" asked Emily uncertainly, her voice echoing slightly.

"Well, we'll be coming out into the back of the garden," said Thomas. "You know, it's sort of dark back there, with all the little trees and bushes and stuff. Don't get all scared now—it will be fine!"

The children swam along, occasionally pushing themselves off the curved walls.

"Shouldn't be far now," said Thomas, still trying to sound breezy and unworried.

"I don't like this one bit," said Emily. "Are you sure it goes all the way through?"

"Okay, here's the problem," said Thomas. "We've come to the end. There must be a grate or something on the bottom that's all clogged with sticks and leaves and stuff, probably everything from the moat that got carried through with all the rain. But look, you can see out a little, up on the top. The garden pool is right on the other side!"

"We can't fit through there!"

"If we pull out some sticks, we can probably climb over."

"Thomas, let's just go back. I really don't like this. I'm getting cold."

"Well, *you* can go back if you want, and *you'll* get in trouble for being outside of the castle at night. I'm going to just pull out a few branches and wriggle through. Then I'll sneak up to my room and be warm and cozy in bed in about ten minutes."

"Does it seem like the water's getting higher?"

"You're just imagining things! And even if the water is rising, the more stuff I pull out, the more water will get through," said Thomas, busily pulling out sticks and clumps of dead leaves from the wall of tangled branches. He threw them past Emily toward the moat. "Wow, this is really hard to pull apart! Probably this big clump's been here a while. There—that should be enough. I'm going to climb over into the pool now. When I get over, you start up and I'll help pull you through."

"Okay, but hurry!"

Thomas began to slowly and awkwardly crawl over the pile of bracken that still clogged the mouth of the tunnel.

"Hurry, Thomas!" yelled Emily. "I think I just felt a fish!"

"Hopefully not a crocodile," said Thomas. A few moments later, he called back to her, "I think I'm sort of stuck. Give me a push, will you?"

"I'll try," she said. "Sort of hard when my feet aren't touching the bottom, you know!" She grabbed onto his feet and shoved as hard as she could.

The pile of sticks and leaves shifted a little, with Thomas on top of it. The front part of him tumbled away out of her sight.

"Thomas! Are you through?" she called, trying to see over the sticks. She couldn't, so she climbed up, squeezing through the top of the pipe. There she could see a bit of

Thomas's lower half, but the top part of him was under-water in the pool!

"*Thomas!*" she screamed, reaching for the one foot she could see. She grabbed it and pulled, but scrambling on the sticks, she had no traction.

Thomas thrashed and lifted his head out of the water and gasped for air. "My other leg's stuck, Emily!" he yelled. "Try and get me out! I can't move—I'll fall back in the water!"

"Can you hold your head up?"

"Yes!" he said, and she thought in a panic that it sounded a bit gurgly. "Hurry, though!"

Emily attacked the pile of sticks, scrabbling frantically and pulling out what she could from the tangled mess. She saw that Thomas's leg was pinned by a branch that must have moved when she first shoved the pile. She pulled at it, but it was held fast by something else. She thrust her hands deeper into the sticks, and through the slime and the mud, her finger-tips touched something smooth and hard. Maybe a stone from the wall had come free and was weighing down the branches. "There's a rock holding it. I have to get it out!"

Emily squeezed through the pipe and managed to wedge

herself against the wall of the pool. Although the water was deeper here, she could work at the stone much easier from her new angle. She rocked it and pulled at it and finally felt it loosen. Just a little more, and her hands could finally wrap all the way around the stone. With a final desperate yank, the stone came loose and a huge part of the pile completely gave way. The water from the pipe surged past, washing years of sticks and branches and leaves and rocks along with it. Thomas and Emily were pushed into the pool along with everything else.

Spluttering, both children climbed out and sat on the stone edge of the pool. "Thanks, Em," said Thomas after a minute or so of coughing up mud. "That was pretty funny, huh?"

"No, it wasn't," said Emily. She was on the grass, holding something and cleaning it with her apron.

"I guess we shouldn't have done that," he said. "Probably should've yelled for Oskar. I guess you were right."

Emily said nothing. Thomas looked over. "Did you not hear me? I said you were right, for the first time in all of recorded history. Why are you cleaning that ridiculous rock?"

She looked up, her face glowing. "You're not going to believe this!"

What she held up triumphantly for Thomas to see was not a rock at all.

It was a trophy.

Chapter Twelve

he children managed to sneak back into the keep without anyone noticing that they were soaked to the skin, that Emily had no shoes, and that she was carrying a very old and cumbersome tennis trophy. They yelled "Good night!" from the dark of the corridor to their grandparents in the den, ran up to Emily's room, shut the door behind them, rushed to her little bedside table, and turned up the flame in her oil lamp.

"Wow," said Thomas, "this thing is really scratched up from the sticks and everything! But there it is: you can read that it says 'Tri-Village Tournament Champions.' It has the names of all the people who won over the years, and the last name I can see is Margaret McThorn!"

"Our Meg!"

"And then, underneath . . . I don't know. I can't really see anything. It's so dirty and all scratched up. I can't tell if it says anything else."

Emily grabbed the trophy from Thomas's hands and furiously rubbed it with her wet apron. "That's better," she said, holding it again in the light. "Now look!"

Underneath Meg's name, in fainter script, someone had etched, as if with a nail, simply and neatly, "and Catherine." Emily handed the trophy to her brother.

"It's really true, what Meg said! She put Mommy's name on it and was going to give it to her, but the dragon took it and—oh, come *on*! You're not going to tell me that you *still* don't believe everything, are you?"

Thomas was studying the trophy intently, holding it gingerly as he turned it to consider all angles. After a minute or so, he looked at his sister, eyes wide.

"You're not going to believe I'm saying this," he said softly. "But I believe it now—I really do. Look at this. These long deep scratches . . . I don't think they were made from sticks! They line up with my fingertips. Something held this. There are two scratches here on the front, one on each side, and six on the back, three on each side. Something with four claws. What has four claws, three in front, one in the back, that could carry a huge trophy like this?"

"A *dragon*! Oh, my goodness, Thomas, it's true!"

Thomas nodded solemnly. "I just don't know what else it could be."

"It's all true, then—the elves and the dragon and fairies and Pomegranate and—"

"Emily, I know you're excited, but we still have to focus here."

"You're right, you're right! The party is tomorrow." Emily got up from where she was crouching on the floor next to the table and began to pace around excitedly. "Having the trophy in person is even better than just old Krackengully being there! The trophy will show for real that the dragon took it and that Meg wasn't lying. Mommy will have no choice but to believe *everything* and want to be friends again!"

"This might be complicated, though," said Thomas. "Getting the trophy to Mother and explaining things when there are hundreds of people around, including Meg."

"Right, right," said Emily, still pacing. "There won't be any time before the party. Lord Gabriel wants everyone, including us, to hide in the Great Hall before they get there so it will be a huge surprise."

"Here's a thought, Emily. It's a party where everyone's bringing presents, right? We'll have Meg give the trophy to her as a present!"

"Great idea, except for one thing: Mommy always says you don't open up the presents in front of everyone at a big party; you save them for later. You know how she is about proper party etiquette! Because what if one person gives you a huge twenty-three-piece crystal punch bowl set, or an antique silver tea service, and then someone else gives you an embroidered handkerchief?"

"What kind of present is a handkerchief? No one better give me a handkerchief as a present."

"I think it would be a very nice present, especially if it had flowers embroidered on it," said Emily, sitting down on the bed.

"Sure, if it was the token a lady gives you before a battle, then it would be all right, I guess."

The children were quiet for a moment as they sat in the near darkness, watching the lamplight flicker and gleam over the battered surface of the trophy. Emily traced one of the dragon's scratches with her fingertip. At last she said, "Mommy's just going to *have* to open it then and there, with Meg right there, too. It's the only way. I think we should wrap it and give it to Mommy ourselves, without Meg even knowing. The trophy *has* to be there—we can't risk her knocking it out a window or forgetting it or leaving it in the storeroom, or anything like that."

"You're still ignoring our biggest obstacle, that Meg said she isn't going to talk to Mother at all," Thomas pointed out.

"She's just going to have to," said Emily. "We'll get her

in that line somehow, by any means possible! And I'm thinking she has to be the very last person!"

"That, at least, will probably not be hard," said Thomas.

"Yes! By the time Mommy gets to Meg, she won't worry about there being a hundred people after her or about opening the present in front of other guests, and she'll have been thinking about what Mr. Krackengully said for at least an hour! She'll be so happy to see Meg that she'll open up the trophy and she'll understand and it will all work out and they'll be friends again and it will be grand, don't you think? And then Meg will be a family friend and she'll come to dinner all the time, and she can bring the other scribes, and it will all be so fun."

"I don't know, Emily," said Thomas. "I know you're trying really hard to make this work, but there's an awful lot of maneuvering of people going on, don't you think? I get the feeling that Meg is kind of hard to maneuver. And even if Krackengully comes, we don't even know what he looks like. How will we get him to stand in the right spot? And then there's Mother! That's a lot of people to fool!"

"We're not fooling them at all! We're just . . . arranging them to be in a certain order, is all. I mean, they were going to go anyway, right? What difference does it make where they stand in line?"

"Yes, but again, what if Meg doesn't like the idea? I don't think we should be trying to trick her. We don't want her to be upset."

"Right, right, because she's a witch," said Emily, lying back on the bed and staring at the ceiling.

"No," said Thomas, "because she's our friend."

When the children pushed open the basement door the next morning, they were greeted by a great bustle of activity as the scribes rushed to finish the last-minute party preparations. They had never seen so much paper and paint! Meg was by the window furiously painting, and the rest of them were wrestling with sheets of colored paper, folding them into great piles of stars and giant beautiful flowers.

"Hi, everyone!" said Thomas, poking his head in. "We knew you'd still have a lot work today, so we came by to see if you needed help!"

"Does it *look* like we need help?" Kitty laughed. "Look, Reggie's ponytail is growing leaves!"

"Oh, great, you got glue in my hair!"

"Don't you little nobles have party things to do?" said Meg, only slightly grumpily. "You must have a very busy day ahead, you know, tuning up your lutes and putting on your special dresses and whatnot."

"We knew you'd be busy," said Emily sweetly. "That's why we're bringing you the biggest basket of goodies ever! We knew you'd all be hungry and cranky today. Consider it a preview for all the treats that will be served tonight."

"I like these kids more all the time!" said Dara, barely visible from under a mountain of flowers. She was trying to fold a menu card so it would stand up by itself on the table. "We're so happy you kids came by! We had a feeling you might, so we have a little surprise for you." She tossed the menu aside and pulled a box out from underneath the table.

"To thank you for all your hard work, helping us out in our time of great need!" said Kitty.

"And for bringing us the treats that have given us the courage to go on," added Reggie.

Meg left her painting and came over to the others. "Yes, yes, it's true, we couldn't have done everything on time without your help! Now open your presents, so everyone can go back to work!" She lifted something tall and pointy and draped with ribbons out of the box. "For you, my dear," she said, handing it to Emily.

"Oh, good grief," said Thomas, laughing.

It was a tall damsel hat, of a very pretty purplish color. "It's just made of paper, so it might only last this one party," Meg explained. "We tried to make it to match your dress, which you described as fuchsia."

"Emily said it was fuchsia so, so many times," said Thomas.

"We used some of that purple ink," said Meg. "If you look really closely, it's white paper but with lots and lots of tiny flowers drawn very small all close together. And we made the veil a nice yellowy green, to be a complementary color."

"It's the most beautiful thing I've ever seen!" said Emily. "Look at the lace trim!"

"And did you notice the lace is really paper? Dara did that herself, cutting out tiny little bits of paper trim with a very sharp knife. Isn't that something?"

"Oh, Dara, thank you! This will be so wonderful tonight with my dress. It will be just perfect!"

Dara beamed. "We ladies of a certain age remember that sometimes the right hat is important for a special party!"

Thomas's gift was a quiver full of arrows that the scribes had made themselves. "Which means you probably shouldn't try to actually shoot them," Lester pointed out.

"But you can draw with them! See? We made them from super-long pencils and pens and even paintbrushes! Because we know you like to write and draw and stuff," said Kitty. "Even if you pretend you don't!"

"And in the middle, in case you didn't notice—" began Meg.

"Ha! My arrow! I *knew* you had it!" said Thomas triumphantly.

Meg laughed. "Of course we did! We had it all along. When you shot it in the window, it flew clear across the room and stuck in the wall! But, now, this is the crazy thing: Reggie had just been holding up some papers, and the arrow pierced them and took them right out of his hands, and wound up tacking the papers right into the wall! It was so useful, we had to keep it for a little while."

"We would hide it when you came in," explained Kitty. "It was extremely stressful."

"And you put my future heraldic device on the quiver!" said Thomas. "Wow!"

"Myrta thought it should just be a lion cub, but we made you a proper lion," said Meg. "We're glad you like your stuff! And now there's *one* last thing you can help me with. Can you help me carry the painting outside? It will never dry in time for tonight if I don't put it out in the sun."

Dara laughed. "Not dry? Uh-oh, someone's going to have a fit!"

"No problem," said Thomas. "It's light. We can do it."

"Watch your fingers. Just hold it by the edges," said Meg

as she held the door for them. "I'll come out in just a second."

"Bye, kids! See you tonight!" called the scribes from their desks.

Outside, the children leaned the painting against the base of the tower. Then they settled themselves down in the grass and waited for Meg.

"I see you brought your coffee," said Emily when Meg appeared. "Does that mean you'll sit out here for a while?"

"I might, seeing as I brought a bunch of your lovely goodies with me!" said Meg, sitting down on the grass with the children and spreading the treats out on an inky cloth.

"And does that mean you're going to tell us the rest of the story?"

"It just might," said Meg. "So, where were we?"

"The dragon was hanging upside down, right in front of Mother," said Thomas.

"Yes," said Emily. "The plan was a disaster so far!"

"Well . . ." Meg began, then paused to nibble a cookie. "Things did not exactly go as planned, but I'm not sure you'd call it a disaster! They did manage to catch the dragon using just a few elves and some tennis nets and bedsheets, which is a pretty amazing accomplishment, when you think about it. And the part with the rope was improvised there on the spot! Still, your mother was in quite a sticky situation. But she wasn't afraid—no, not her!"

"Do you think maybe Mommy wasn't afraid the dragon would roast her because, well, they weren't exactly friends, but he had been at least a little bit nice to her, right?" said Emily cautiously. "I mean, he brought her blankets and soup and muffins—that's something, isn't it?"

"Maybe that did have something to do with it," Meg said thoughtfully. "Perhaps your mother did think that the dragon had a heart somewhere underneath all his scales. And I agree, someone who brings you soup and muffins is probably not all bad! But dragons are very unpredictable. Even though your mother hoped for the best, she knew she couldn't trust him. Not yet.

"She stood in her window, bravely facing the dragon head-on. No one down below could quite see what was happening, but the elves who were lashed to the dragon could. And your mother spoke in a clear, loud voice so that everyone could hear. And this is what she said: 'Dragon! You find yourself in a precarious position, as do I. Our lives, and the lives of the elves, hang in the balance. But if you hold your fiery breath and agree to our demands, your captors will let you down gently.'

"She waited. The dragon narrowed his terrible red eyes, which burned with an angry and suspicious yet fearful light. Wisps of smoke began to curl from his nostrils. Your mother was still unafraid, though. She spoke again: 'If you do not agree, then roast me with your terrible flames. But if you do that, the knights will let go of the rope that holds you, and you will plummet to the ground, unable to use your wings. Even if you survive that fall, Dragon, one thing is for certain.' And here your mother lifted up a long paper covered with strange makings for him to see. 'You will never know what is written in this letter! Will you hold your fiery breath, Dragon, so I may read it to you?'

"Even upside down, the dragon knew what it was. Even upside down, Catherine saw him give her a barely perceptible nod, and saw that his eyes lost just a tiny bit of their anger—just a little! She put the paper down, then picked up another, a more human-size piece. It was her translation of the letter that had come in the envelope that Acorn had been wearing—the letter your father helped with by going to the library and looking words up, if you remember all that! And this is what the letter said:

Dearest one, *my sweet Dragon,*

Do you remember me, *the friend of your youth?*
The days we played and flew together were the
happiest of my life. The day my family took me away,
when there was not time even to say goodbye, broke
my heart, and has filled me with pain all these long
years. To never see you again, my dearest friend,
would mean only an empty life of sadness.
  Maybe now that we are grown there is a way,
though we are far from each other. Can I only dream of
a time when we see each other again, to fly and touch
our claws together? Can I dream also that you remember
me with love? My heart trembles with a joy long forgotten,
to imagine it can be. Please write to me, my dear one.
I am waiting for your answer.
  If this letter has not found you, or you wish to be
left alone, I will continue to live, but the fire in my
basilisk heart will finally burn out. Please write back
to me, my love, and tell me there is hope.

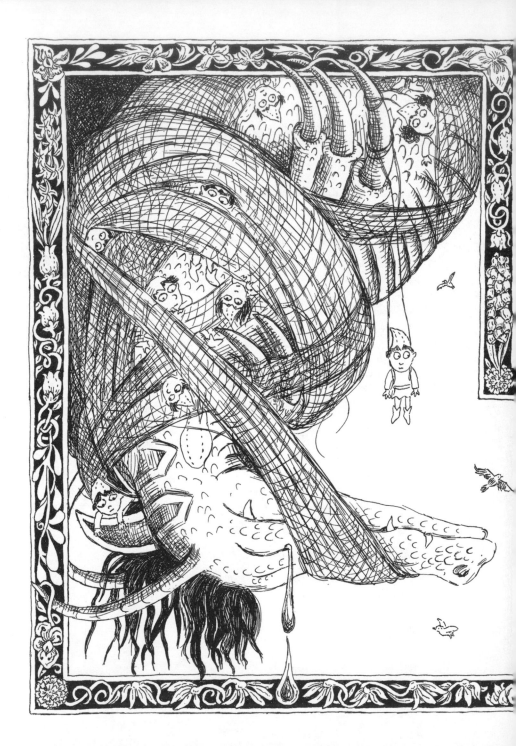

"'The letter is signed with love,' Catherine said, 'but it is a name I cannot translate. There is no word for it in the book. But you know who it's from, don't you?'

"The dragon nodded, and his eyes were not angry or suspicious at all anymore. In fact, his eyes were closed. Tears rolled from the corners of his eyes and fell to the ground, and no smoke came from his nostrils. Even though your mother knew the dragon was deeply affected by the letter, she knew she had to get to the rest of the plan. She still didn't completely trust him."

"Dragons are indeed wily beasts," Thomas agreed. "Fully capable of using false tears for effect, to treacherously gain the trust of their opponent."

"I have heard that said of crocodiles as well," said Meg. "There are indeed many similarities. But right now we are only worried about this one large, heartsick, but possibly still wily, dragon. Your mother told him that there were conditions. He had to let her go, and all the knights and horses, too. And never lock anyone up again. And stop scaring the villagers and stealing their things and stop trying to eat the elves. (This one made him narrow his eyes again and the teeniest bit of smoke drifted out of his nose.) And if he went back on his word, well, here Catherine waved her hand at a crow sitting at the top of the beech tree in the meadow. She said the crow had the envelope with the basilisk's return address and was ready to fly and drop it into the middle of the deepest lake if there was any trouble. So the dragon agreed! And they gently let him down, and the knights came and cut away all the nets with their swords, and the elves were all freed. And the dragon sent Jerry to unlock Catherine from the tower, and she came down."

"And everyone was friends?" asked Emily, eyes shining.

"Well, it was the beginning of being friends, I guess you could say," said Meg.

"But something else must have happened," said Emily. "Since the dragon used to live here but now he doesn't anymore."

"You are quite right. There's just a little bit more, if you can stand it! The dragon really was as good as his word; he didn't roast anyone at all. And he honestly felt quite bad about everything, frightening everyone for so long, and especially locking your mother in the tower! Catherine saw that he really was trying so hard to be a good dragon, so she offered to help him."

"Help him what?" asked Thomas.

"What the dragon really wanted was for Catherine to help him write a letter."

"To his childhood sweetheart, the basilisk!" said Emily.

"What an astute young lady you are! Yes, he wanted Catherine to help him write a letter in Basilisk, which, by now, she knew quite well."

"Did he have to write it himself, with a pencil? That must've been hard, with his big claws!"

"Oh, it was, but he wanted to!"

"And did he sit at a tiny desk with a piece of paper, just like we do at our lessons?"

"Yes! It was really funny, a big dragon sitting at a little desk, with your mother as the teacher! And when the letter was ready to be sent, the elves sent along a flattering portrait they painted themselves. Maybe they made him out to be a little more handsome than in real life, but who knows? So hard to tell with the larger reptiles, don't you think? And your mother made a large basilisk-size hankie from the last bit of bedsheet that had not been made into a parachute, embroidered with the wildflowers of the meadow. In the olden days, that's what would've been called a token of love, you know."

"Well, they still do stuff like that," said Thomas. "Ladies give knights things before a tournament or when they go into battle."

"Which Thomas knows from his knight studies," said Emily.

"Though the dragon had already lost one battle," Meg said, "they were hoping he would win the next: the battle for the basilisk's scaly, reptilian heart!"

"You know, the story got really good there for a while," said Thomas, "but now it's going downhill again."

"Well, lucky for you it's nearly ended," said Meg. "And that really is about all there is. They sent the letter, and off it went to whatever faraway land the basilisk lived in. And soon after, another letter came, and the dragon flew away, so I guess the reply was favorable. Maybe by then the dragon could read it himself, and your mother didn't have to translate. You'll have to ask her. Anyway, that was that. But before he flew away, never to be seen again, the dragon gave your mother the castle in gratitude for all her help. He simply didn't need it anymore."

"And Mommy and Daddy got married!"

"Yes, but not right off, of course. You had to have a

proper long engagement back then, you know, unlike the impulsive young people of today! And there was so much to be done. They gave back all the things the dragon had stolen from people, and had a huge yard sale to get rid of some of the dragon's furniture—some of it was just entirely too big, you know. And your mother and grandmother had to sew new curtains and make tablecloths. Oh, and Catherine had to finish damsel college! So it was quite some time, a year at least! But, yes, then they got married and that was that."

"And they lived here and they had us and now they're having their anniversary!"

"Isn't it so funny how it all worked out?" said Meg. "Maybe tonight at the party they'll have a toast and someone will ask them how they met. Do you think they'll say?"

"Wouldn't that be funny!"

"Who knows? Maybe I'll even ask it myself!"

"Oh, Meg! You *are* going to make up with Mommy! I *knew* you would! And you really want to? It isn't just because—?"

"Because Emily's so pushy and annoying, you couldn't take it anymore?" asked Thomas.

Meg laughed. "Well, she is, a little."

"A *lot*," said Thomas.

"Maybe so, but it's because she has a big heart. I know she can't help herself. And"—Meg sighed—"I do see that, looking at events now after all these years, that perhaps there is a possibility that I could look at them in a different way. And telling this story makes me remember just how much I do miss my friend." She took a long sip of her coffee.

The three of them sat for a few more minutes in the grass, eating treats and enjoying the sunshine.

"I like that you gave Mommy a crown of flowers in her picture," said Emily. "Do you think that's really what she wore?"

"I have no idea—I wasn't there," said Meg, but she was smiling when she said it.

"It's very pretty," said Emily.

"I thought she'd like it," said Meg. "No one could really remember, and I thought it would look nice."

"It's like the one I made you yesterday."

"It is," said Meg. "I'm sorry I forgot it."

"I made you another," said Emily. "While I was sitting here. Lots of flowers in the grass, you know."

"Thank you. I'll wear it tonight," said Meg, taking another sip of her coffee.

Chapter Thirteen

mily, *shhh*!" Thomas whispered to his sister as the two of them crouched behind a huge armchair right next to the door of the Great Hall. They, along with hundreds of other party guests, were doing their best to be, as Lord Gabriel had told them, as quiet as mice.

"But where *are* the children?" they heard their mother ask from the kitchen behind the door.

"I think I saw them go in there, stealin' cookies and spoilin' their dinner as usual" was the cook's sour, muffled reply.

Emily, who was immensely enjoying her mother's perplexed tone, stifled a giggle.

She, along with everyone else, didn't have much longer to keep quiet. They heard footsteps approach the door, which was then slowly pushed open. Catherine and Stephen stood in the doorway, looking tired and confused.

"SURPRISE!" shouted the great crowd of people assembled in the hall as they all burst from their hiding places in a thunderous wave of applause and cheering. Emily was thrilled to see the look of delight appear on her mother's face. The Great Hall had never looked so grand. Bright, festive banners hung from the ceiling to the floor, and the windows and tables were festooned with colorful buntings. The wedding painting was finished and looked magnificent, displayed on a table with an abundance of colorful flowers all around it. More flowers covered the dining tables, which were set with the most sumptuous linens and silver, and torches blazed from the walls. Most wonderful, though, were the people: hundreds of guests, all happy, all cheering and laughing in their most beautifully colored clothes, in the most brilliant, shiniest, and fashionable fabrics. It was almost dizzying. Closest to Thomas, Emily, and their parents were their extended family: grandparents, aunts, uncles, and cousins, many they hadn't seen in ages, then people from the castle, then farther back, people they knew from the village, but also many they did not. So many faces! The room was completely stuffed.

Thomas and Emily ran to their parents and hugged them. "Are you surprised?" Emily asked.

"Oh, yes!" her mother said with a laugh. "I can't believe how amazing everything looks! This is absolutely wonderful!"

Emily tried to tell her that they helped with the invitations, and that they had met Meg, but the music started at once, and the crowd began to form a long, noisy line as people waited their turn to embrace Catherine and Stephen and give them their best wishes. Some had gifts, which they put on the table that held the wedding painting. (Emily and Thomas had wrapped their gift, the trophy, and stashed it behind the painting for safekeeping.) The children stayed with their parents while they were greeted by their family and some of the castle people, then Thomas steered Emily away.

"I think we've had enough of that hugging and kissing from relatives business," he said, wiping his face. "Bleccchhhh! Let's go find the scribes! You know where they'll be."

"Skulking in the back by the snack table!" said Emily. "But remember the plan? People are getting in line already— we have to find Mr. Krackengully."

"How are we going to recognize him?"

"Well, he'll be someone we don't know, someone old, someone who looks like he doesn't really know anyone, I guess."

"There's a lot of old people we've never met before

here," said Thomas. "Let's just go find the scribes first. And remember: we have the trophy, so Mr. Krackengully might not even matter so much anyway."

They pushed their way through the noisy crowd, nibbling here and there at the plates of appetizers held out by serving people. People all around them were talking and eating and drinking and laughing, and the music seemed to come from all directions. There were jugglers and magicians and singers to amuse guests while they waited in line. Emily kept looking for someone who might be Mr. Krackengully. She began to nervously wonder if he wasn't here yet. What if he hadn't come at all?

Eventually they found themselves at the back of the hall, where, just as they thought, the scribes were busily loading up little plates from one of the tables.

"Oh, look at you in your hat! Such a proper young lady!" said Dara, giving Emily a hug.

"Hi, everyone!" said Thomas.

"This is the best party I think they've ever had here!" said Lester.

"Definitely with the best food," said Kitty. "And look at this crazy thing we helped make: a big mama pineapple crocodile, surrounded by baby pineapple crocodiles!"

"It was my idea," said Reggie proudly. "We gave them bloodthirsty red cherry eyes, even the babies. Nice, don't you think?"

"Oh, they're adorable! And you all look spectacular!" said Emily. "But where's Meg? Don't tell me she didn't come! Oh, Thomas, she didn't come—I can't believe it!"

"Don't worry, kids, Meg's here!" said Myrta. "She was excited to come, really!"

"I lent her the dress I made for the Cabbage Festival," said Kitty. "It looks smashing on her! She probably went off looking for the court astronomer."

"Oh, okay. Great!" said Emily. It was a little quieter here in the back, away from the bustling line of noisy guests. While they nibbled on some of the delicious and clever appetizers, the children chatted with the scribes about what they were going to do next week since they were all done with the party things. Emily began to relax.

Just then Kitty said, "Well, would you look who it is!"

Emily turned in relief, expecting to see Meg, but was instead met with a sullen-looking teenage boy.

"Hey," he said.

"This is Wat, our proper apprentice," said Reggie.

"Not that he's been apprenticing much lately," observed Myrta.

"Figures he shows up for the party, though!" said Kitty.

Wat's ears went bright red. "So, uh, I just saw Meg, and she told me to tell you guys not to eat all the crocodiles. She said to save her one."

"Meg? She's here? You just saw her?" said Emily.

"Uh-huh. I didn't talk to her long, though," Wat said peevishly. "She said she was busy trying to think of stuff to say—something about 'getting it over with.' Then she totally kicked me out of the line and told me to come back here—"

"*What?* Meg's in line already?" said Emily. She dropped her uneaten baby pineapple crocodile and grabbed Thomas's hand, pulling him after her back into the crowd. "We have to forget about finding Mr. Krackengully. We need to find Meg! Who knows what could happen if she gets to Mommy before we give her the trophy? Who knows what she'll say? We can't let them talk alone. Meg could ruin everything!"

The children tried to make their way up to the front of the hall, but pushing through the crowd turned out to be a slow business. There were tables covered in precariously balanced arrangements of fruit and flowers to get around, jugglers to avoid, and, most dangerous of all, relatives grabbing them for enthusiastic hugs. "Oh, don't you two just look so grown up, and look at you in your precious hat! Such a little lady! Why, I haven't seen you since you were this high!" said one distant, barely remembered auntie after the next.

"You *had* to wear the hat," grumbled Thomas when they freed themselves for the third time.

"Come on, we have to keep going!" said Emily, shaking off a tiny cousin. "I don't see Meg anywhere!"

They were nearly at the front of the hall when they spotted Meg in the line. She was dangerously close to their mother—not more than ten people away!

"Meg! You're here!" said Emily, slowing down and sliding into the line with Thomas. "Look at your beautiful dress!"

"Why, thank you, young miss," said Meg, looking genuinely pleased and dropping into a curtsy. "Look, I practiced curtsying, in honor of the occasion, in case I run into some proper grown-up nobles. Don't you look charming!"

"So, Meg," said Emily, trying her best to sound casual, "Thomas and I were just talking to the other scribes in back, and, uh, they talked some of the musicians into playing the Otter Gavotte, and, uh, Reggie said if we had enough people, we could start our own Otter Gavotte circle, but Thomas needs a partner, right, Thomas? He really wants to learn it!"

"Uh, yeah, I do!" said Thomas. "Knights have to know all this courtly dance stuff . . . I guess."

"Isn't that nice!" said Meg. "Of course you should learn the Otter Gavotte! I know it well. We all had to learn the courtly dances back in my day, you know."

"Yes, yes, unlike us poorly educated wretches of today," said Emily quickly, hurrying things along.

"Tell the gang I'll be there in a minute. I've been waiting in line all this time, so I don't want to get out. Look, I'm almost up to your mother!"

"Oh, you can talk to her later!" said Emily with a dismissive wave of her hand. "She'll be here all night! Wouldn't it be more fun to dance first?"

"I haven't eaten a thing yet, and I can't dance on an empty stomach!" Meg protested. "Talk first, then eat, then dance, then more talking! That's the best order for a party. Besides, if I don't talk with your mother now, I may not get to talk to her for hours! Best to do it now while my courage is up, you know? I'm going to apologize for being such a brat when I was a kid and make things right, just like we talked about."

Emily nervously looked up at the line—only seven people to her mother now! She turned to her brother. "Say, uh,

Thomas," she said, shoving him as gently as possible in the direction of the table that held the presents, "why don't you go, uh, find us some punch, for Meg and me to have while we wait?"

"Huh?"

"I've already had at least three cups," said Meg. "Any more and I'll have to get out of the line, if you get what I'm saying here."

"Well, get me some," said Emily.

"Emily, I don't really think this is a good time—"

"You know, a *really big cup* of punch?"

"Oh, yeah, uh, sure! Punch, right!"

She turned back to Meg, who looked suspicious. "Is there suddenly a reason you don't want me to talk to your mother?" she said.

"Oh, no, not at all!" said Emily. They were only three people away now. Emily tried not to look at Thomas, who was making a complete mess of the gift table, tossing presents this way and that. "It's just that, well, maybe the line isn't the best place to do this. You know, so many people around—maybe the time between dinner and dessert would be better. You could sit up with us at the fancy head table!

That would be fun. We always get the best food, you know—"

"Look, I'm going to talk to your mother. It's going to be fine. I'm ready to be friends again. Thanks for caring so much about this—I really appreciate it, okay? Now run back and tell the gang I'll be there in a few minutes!"

She shooed Emily away, and not knowing what else to do, Emily joined Thomas in furiously rummaging through the gifts. "We have to find it, Thomas!" she said. "Meg is almost to Mommy!"

"I know, I know!" said Thomas. "I put it right here behind the painting! Where is it?"

"Be careful! You're going to knock the painting over! Oh, hurry! Look underneath the table. Maybe it fell behind. I'll hold the painting up. Oh, my goodness, it's still wet! I got paint on my new dress! And if Mommy sees us going through the presents, she'll be mortified!"

"Calm down, Emily!" said Thomas, his muffled voice coming from under the table. "I knew this was a dumb idea."

"Hurry! Mommy is talking to the person right before Meg. Please, please, keep talking! Oh, no, now they're hugging—hurry!"

"Okay, here it is! Take it!" Thomas pushed the trophy, wrapped in all sorts of cast-off paper and ribbons, out from underneath the tablecloth. Emily grabbed it, straightened up, and walked as quickly and gracefully as she could to the front of the line, where Meg and her mother were already talking. Her father was turned away, talking to some other people. Thomas crawled out from under the table as inconspicuously as possible and followed.

"Well, if it isn't my old friend Meg," Emily heard her mother say. As she came around to where they were standing, she was relieved to see they were clasping hands. Not exactly hugging, like her mother had done with so many others, but a good sign! Still, she wondered uneasily, was her mother's smile a little uncertain? Was she not happy? Maybe she was just tired from having to hug and kiss a hundred people before Meg?

"How very good of you to come. It's been a long time."

"Yes, it has," said Meg. "And I must tell you it was your children's idea. We've, uh . . . become pretty good friends this week, it seems."

"Have you?" said their mother. She was definitely smiling, maybe a tiny bit stiffly, but then again perhaps not. Emily wasn't sure. "I'm really happy to hear that!"

"Yes, Mommy!" said Emily, thinking that this was the perfect opportunity to insert herself and Thomas into the conversation. "We met Meg and all the scribes and we helped make the invitations and the name cards and we've been working every day and—"

"Working every day?" repeated her mother, raising an eyebrow just slightly.

"Uh, well, I wouldn't say they were *working* exactly. Just visiting and keeping us company, more like playing really," Meg began.

"Oh, yes, we went every day!" added Emily quickly. "It's been fun! We weren't playing, though—we were really helping with everything!"

"Meg never made us—we wanted to!" added Thomas. "We wanted to keep up with our penmanship and—"

"And Meg told us the most wonderful story about—"

"I see," said their mother, her smile definitely frozen now, her tone frosty. "Telling my children stories. Well, that's our Meg, isn't it, with her fabulous tales? I can't wait to hear them."

Emily felt her face getting hot. Her mother's voice was definitely on the edge of being angry. This wasn't how it was supposed to go! Quickly she pushed the trophy into her mother's hands.

"Look, Mommy! Meg got you an anniversary present, and doesn't it look nice? Why not open it?"

"I most certainly did not get you a present," said Meg,

who was starting to sound annoyed, "because I wasn't actually even *invited*. I just came because—"

"It was a *surprise party*," said Catherine rather forcefully. "I didn't invite anyone!"

"Just like you didn't invite me to your *wedding*!"

"How can you say that? Of course I did! You never sent your reply card back! And after I wrote you a special personal apology for not believing you, which you utterly ignored! I thought I would do the mature thing and try to start anew, but clearly you didn't want to—"

"Please, Mommy!" said Emily. "Meg said the mail was worse in the olden days! Maybe it never came!"

"As usual, Meg has an excuse for everything! What did she say, a goblin ate it?"

"Don't you want to see the present Meg gave you?" said Emily, desperately trying to change the subject. "It will explain everything!" She awkwardly tried to unwrap the trophy even as her mother held it, but the ribbons were knotted very tightly ('Knot tying is an important skill for knights,' she remembered Thomas saying, now regretting the knot-tying contest that had ensued), and her mother was paying no attention anyway. Emily found herself talking very quickly and very loudly so she could be heard above the arguing women. "You *have* to see what it is, Mommy. You will be so surprised and you'll love it! It will explain everything! Thomas and I found it in the moat and—"

"*The moat!* What are you talking about? You sent my children into *the moat*? What's been going on here?"

"I have no idea what they're talking about—I mean it!" Meg looked stricken.

"It's true, Mother!" said Thomas, jumping in. "Meg had no idea we went into the moat last night!"

"*The moat at night!* How *dare* you put my children in harm's way!" Catherine was so angry now that she stepped toward Meg, and the trophy, still wrapped, went flying. Emily dashed after it.

"I had a feeling the children would run into you some-day, Meg, and I did think they would enjoy your—your youthful spirit! It wasn't enough to fill their heads with your ridiculous stories, though, was it? Because now I hear you've been making them do work and go into the moat! How utterly irresponsible of you, and I have to say, I am not at all surprised!"

"I never made them do anything! Swimming in the moat was their idea!"

"Oh, so now my children are liars, I suppose? How like you, Meg, to blame everyone else, so childish and irrespon-sible, as usual!"

"Irresponsible, ha! Funny to hear that coming from you. *You* were the one who abandoned your team at the most important time *ever*!"

"I cannot *believe* you're bringing that up after all these years!"

Emily came back, trophy in hand. It was still wrapped, but the ribbons were hanging off it now. She felt foolish, clutching it forlornly and not knowing what to do. With a sinking feeling, she noticed that a circle of curious onlook-ers, including her father, had begun to form around the women, who were now, she had to admit, screaming freely at each other. Thomas had retreated. He came and stood next to her. They looked at each other hopelessly.

"I think we can officially say this is not going as planned," he said.

"Oh, you think?" said Emily miserably. She could barely make out what they were saying anymore. It almost didn't matter. Everything was ruined.

Chapter Fourteen

he room grew strangely quiet as more and more guests seemed to notice that something at the party was not quite right. People stopped their own conversations and began to listen in curiously to the two women. Laughter and music began to trail away. An anxious hush fell over the room, and only Meg's and Catherine's voices could be heard.

"I'm actually *glad* you didn't show up! I could always play better than you anyway. You never could get anything even close to the line! I always had to do everything—"

"How dare you say that! Everyone knew I was the stronger player! In fact that's why Krackengully made me play with you—I never even wanted you for a partner! He said you had potential, which, of course, you squandered, but you needed help and you should be paired with someone a lot better—"

"He did not! He told me—"

"We have to do something!" Emily whispered to her brother in alarm, but he only shrugged hopelessly and looked down at his feet.

"There's only one way to settle this!" shouted Meg. "Get your racket!"

"You're on!"

Catherine abruptly turned on her heels and swept through the crowd toward the door that led to the kitchen. Emily started after her. "Mommy, no! This is all a mistake. Meg was coming to be friends again!"

"Too late for that!" said her mother, already through the door. She slammed it behind her.

Meg had stomped off, too. Thomas was standing next to his father with his mouth open in shock. He couldn't have looked more surprised if someone had smacked him in the face with a dead fish.

"Was that *our* mother?" he said. "Who left her own fancy party for a grudge tennis match?"

"Daddy!" said Emily. "Can't you make Mommy be sensible?"

Her father also looked like someone had smacked him in

the face with a dead fish. He only said, "I think this one is out of our hands, my dear."

"But what are we going to *do?*" Emily wailed. "The beautiful party . . ." She looked around helplessly. All the bright colors, the dresses and the banners and the buntings, seemed to swim and swirl before her eyes, and the confusing buzz of noise had started up again. She couldn't bear to look into the faces of the guests. What if they were shocked or confused or upset or even angry? What would all the relatives think? Did they know it had all been her fault, ruining the party?

A large hand clasped her shoulder. She looked up, and Lord Gabriel was grinning hugely at her. "Isn't this *amazing*?"

"What?"

"Don't you worry, young Miss Emily! People are going to *love* this! This party will be the talk of the village for years! It's gonna be fabulous. Always remember: a good party can turn on a dime!"

"But I don't understand. It's all ruined!"

Lord Gabriel was actually laughing. "No, it isn't! Listen to what people are saying! This is *great*!"

Emily looked into the crowd and saw that people were smiling and laughing and chattering excitedly. She heard murmurs of "Oh, a change in venue! How absolutely cunning!" and "What fun—a tennis match!" and "An outdoor party in the woods, how exquisite! Oh, Lord Gabriel, you have truly outdone yourself!"

He turned to bark orders at some of the servers, then turned back to Emily and Thomas. "Hey, can you kids help me out here? You know where the tennis courts are, don't you? How about you run along ahead and warn old Crankypants that the party's coming? We're going to start packing all the food and flowers and everything up." He grabbed some torches off the wall and gave them to the children. "You'd better get going! We'll be along as quick as we can!" He turned back to the servers. "Hey, watch that painting! It's still wet, isn't it? I knew it would be—*Meg*! Oh, wait, she left, right?"

"Well! It seems to me you two have had an interesting week!" said Stephen. "I'm not really sure what's going on, but I guess you two should go. I'll go find your mother and walk with her."

Thomas and Emily ran off with their torches. It wasn't until they were over the drawbridge and well into the trees that they turned to look at the procession that had started to form behind them. If the woods had seemed a little spooky in the darkness just the night before, it was a completely different picture now, with the torches bobbing like a cheerful line of enormous friendly fireflies, and the talk and laughter as the ladies hitched up their long skirts and picked their way delicately down the path. Some took off their shoes and laughed at the feel of the cool, soft moss and pine needles. All the lights and the noise made it jolly and fun, and some of the musicians even played and sang as they walked. At the end came Lord Gabriel and all the servants pulling wagons loaded with food and drinks and flowers.

"Wow, they're all really coming!" said Emily.

"And they're coming faster than I would've thought," said Thomas. "I guess they really do like this idea! Let's hurry, Emily, and help get things ready."

They sped down the path. When they were about halfway to the tennis courts, they saw the light of a torch bobbing slowly and uncertainly toward them from the opposite way. The children slowed to a walk. "I'll bet it's Mr. Krackengully!" Thomas said to Emily. "I forgot all about him in the excitement!"

"Are you sure?" whispered Emily. "Maybe pixies carry torches."

"It's him," said Thomas. "Look, the torch is at grown-up height."

Eventually the bearer of the torch emerged from the darkness, and it was indeed an older man, dressed quite nattily in the fashion of a day gone by, his long white hair pulled back into a ponytail. He seemed surprised and even a little alarmed at the presence of the children. He stopped and peered at them from underneath great bushy white eyebrows.

Emily spoke first. "Um, hello . . . Mr. Krackengully, sir?"

The old man's eyes narrowed. "How do you know my name?" he said, sounding not at all pleased. "Don't tell me you're those little hooligans from the village coming back to wreck my tennis courts again! Haven't you caused me enough trouble?"

"What? No, we're not!" said Thomas. "We're from the castle, and—"

"The castle! What a coincidence: I'm on my way to a party at the castle right now. I've got the invitation right here."

"The party isn't at the castle anymore!" Emily burst out. "It's on its way here right now. They want to play tennis! It's a match—"

"No party at the castle tonight?" said Mr. Krackengully, a look of confusion spreading over his face. "Was the invitation some kind of joke? I thought it seemed a bit short notice but—"

"No, sir, it wasn't a joke at all!" said Thomas. "There's a party, but it's coming here!"

"Hundreds of people are on their way right now!" said Emily. "We know this sounds crazy, but you don't mind, do you? Two people are going to have a tennis match. You'll remember them from when they were girls! One is Margaret McThorn."

"Margaret McThorn, Margaret McThorn," murmured Mr. Krackengully, his eyes searching the trees. "Oh, you mean little Meggy! She was a sprite, that one. Never did see—"

"We can talk about Meg later!" said Thomas. "We really have to get the courts ready, sir! If you don't mind us going to clear the leaves off."

"Oh, no, go right ahead! I could use some help! So, a tennis tournament tonight, no party? I got all dressed up for nothing?"

"There's going to be a party here very soon! Hundreds of people!" said Emily.

"Well, I don't think I have enough food to feed that many. I'll have to check the root cellar . . ."

"Don't worry, they're bringing the food! If you wait here, they'll be right along! Thomas and I have to go get ready!"

"Well, you run along and do that, then," said Mr. Krackengully, sitting down on a tree stump. "I'll just wait here for the big party!"

The children raced on ahead, up the hill and along the ridge and then down the slope. When they got to the courts, they stuck their torches into the ground, and Thomas immediately found a rake in the shed and started to furiously clean away the dead leaves. Emily found some string and quickly began to fashion a makeshift net by tying lots of smaller pieces of string to two long pieces strung between the poles.

"You were right: this could be a disaster!" she said as she tied knot after knot. "What if it gets worse?"

"I'm not sure it can, and like Father said, it's out of our hands. I think the important thing is that in the end it's a good party, like Lord Gabriel thinks it will be. And that Mother and Meg don't have a fistfight. That's the best we can hope for," said Thomas as he raked.

The scribes arrived first, rushing down the slope together.

"We ran as fast as we could!" said Lester, out of breath. "What should we do to help get ready?"

"Put some of your torches into the path where it comes down the hill. It's steep and we don't want anyone falling," said Thomas. "Then come help me with the leaves."

"Shouldn't Meg be with you?" Emily asked.

"She had to find her racket!" said Myrta, crouching down to help with the knot tying.

Reggie came to help with the net, too. "Who knows how long that will take," he said. "I think it's down in the store-room, way in back. I don't know the last time we saw it! She could be a while."

Soon children from the castle came scrambling down the

hill, laughing and shouting, happy and excited to be allowed to run and play in the woods at night, and in their good clothes, even! More and more guests emerged from the trees after them, most picking their way more carefully. They set their torches by the courts, which illuminated them quite beautifully. The musicians came and arranged themselves in a bunch on one side of the court, and soon Lord Gabriel was there, too, with all the servants and the wagons. He immediately started ordering them to set up the food and drinks on the other court.

Thomas and Emily sat down on the sidelines with the scribes.

"I'm so nervous!" Emily told Thomas. "I'm not sure who I should be rooting for!"

"There's Meg!" said Reggie. "Hey, Meg! Over here!"

Meg took no notice of her friends but took her place on one side of the court across from Catherine. The crowd settled down, and out to the center of the courts came Mr. Krackengully. "Thank you all for coming!" he announced, and the crowd cheered politely. "It is my great honor to officiate at this match of two of my favorite students! Let's have this be a fair game, kids! Meg, you won the last game, so you serve first." He tossed her a ball, and then went to sit at the sidelines with everyone else.

Meg, her face set and her eyes steely, served.

Except she didn't.

"You missed," said Catherine crisply. "I'm not surprised. You're clearly out of practice."

Meg tried again, and missed again.

"Give it another go," said Catherine. Meg did, and missed.

"You're not tossing the ball high enough."

"I am so!"

"And bend your knees more."

"You're still bossy!" Meg yelled from her side of the court. "Bossy, bossy, bossy!"

"You're still a terrible server!" Catherine yelled back.

"Oh, yeah? I'll show you terrible serving!" said Meg, tossing the ball high into the air and swinging her racket hard. She hit the ball this time, straight and fast, right at Catherine. The crowd gasped.

"I can't look!" whispered Emily to Thomas as she covered her eyes.

"Yikes—she knocked her hat right off!" said Thomas.

"Oh, no, they're going to fight again!" said Emily. "I can't take this."

"Sorry," Meg called over. "That was a mistake."

"You did that on purpose!"

"I did not! You shouldn't have been wearing it anyway—that's a stupid hat for tennis! You should have a fashionable flower crown like mine. It's what everyone's wearing now, much more sporty!"

Emily, who had been fearing the worst, heard a smile in Meg's voice. Then there was the sound of the ball bouncing back and forth. When she heard Meg laughing, and her mother laughing, too, she knew it was safe to open her eyes.

The game didn't last long. Neither Catherine nor Meg actually managed to hit the ball all that often, and when they did, it usually went sailing into the crowd. Finally Meg hit the ball straight up into the tree branches that hung over the court and it never came back down. She made a great show of curtsying elegantly to Catherine, and said "You win!" Then they ran to each other and hugged. The crowd went wild with cheers.

Lord Gabriel stepped onto the court and quieted the applause, suggesting that since everyone was already arranged so nicely, why didn't they have some entertainment while the food was being made ready? And Meg and Catherine sat down with Stephen, and the musicians started up again, and Emily found her friends and they did their special dance, and Thomas borrowed a lute and played his solo. Emily thought she saw her mother crying, but in a good way.

The party went deep into the night. After dinner there was dancing on one of the courts and tennis on the other. Mr. Krackengully found a bunch of rackets in the shed and started giving lessons and signing people up for more next week. Thomas and Emily had a marvelous time dancing the Otter Gavotte with the scribes and playing with the other kids from the castle and the village. In the middle of a game, they stumbled over Meg, who was sitting on the grass by the courts with their parents.

"Hey, kids!" said Meg. "You should see this! Your mother thinks she can still do a cartwheel! This should be good."

"We can't—we're in the middle of playing knights and dragons!" called Emily as she ran past and into the woods with the other kids. When she was as far into the trees as she thought she should go, she stopped for a moment and stood listening, wanting to remember this beautiful night forever. Though music and singing and shouting filled the air, if she listened hard, she could still hear the other sounds of the night, the wilder sounds, birds and insects and the wind rustling the leaves and then . . . Was that the sound of tiny bells ringing? Or could that possibly be the very faint sound of elvish laughter? Or even the beating wings of a beast come to visit an old friend? Emily knew there was no way to be sure, not at a noisy and absolutely wonderful party like this! She turned and ran back to the lights and the music and the tennis courts. "Wait up, Thomas!" she called. "I'm going to be a dragon next!"

The End